arthur's
room

Arthur's spirit struggles to escape
the cage of cerebral palsy

Cynthia Davidson Bend

www.cynthiabend.dgi.bz

Beaver's Pond Press, Inc.
Edina, Minnesota

ISBN 1-931646-34-1

Library of Congress Catalog Number: 2002090389

Printed in the United States of America

First Printing: March 2002

06 05 04 03 02   6 5 4 3 2 1

5125 Danen's Drive
Edina, MN 55439-1465
(952) 829-8818
www.beaverspondpress.com

to order, visit midwestbookhouse.com or call 1-877-430-0044. Quantity discounts available.

To my husband, Meredith, with loving
thanks for supporting me through the years it
took to complete *Arthur's Room* and for his
meticulous editing of the final draft.

Acknowledgements

My love and my thanks go first to my playwright father, Bill Davidson, who is responsible for my decision in sixth grade to become a writer.

I am indebted to my husband's brother, Bradford Bend, severely disabled by cerebral palsy, for teaching me to admire and respect his ability and that of his family to make loving lives for each other.

I am grateful to Prof. Harold Alford, Ph.D. not only for his patient encouragement and critiques through the first drafts of *Arthur's Room*, but for his role in co-founding The School For Social Development (now Partnership Resources.)

I was introduced to Lucy Walsh by a near collision as I was swimming across May's Lake. To prevent my colliding with her rowboat, Lucy put her hand on my head. We had a substantive conversation as I tread water. When she was called to shore for a barbecue she said, "Come to school, or I may never see you again." I visited the School For Social Development, and I co-taught for eight years with my dear friend and mentor, Lucy Walsh.

Without the patience, courage, and hard work which my special students, Richard and David demonstrated, *Arthur's Room* would have been impossible. David, I thank you for fantasy and humor. Richard, I thank you for your friendship and for honesty, trust, insight and persistent work.

I am grateful to my indefatigable readers, June Beck and Clelia Mulally who have repeatedly critiqued *Arthur's Room* and encouraged me through more drafts than I can count. June has been connected with our writing family ever since she acted in one of my father's plays while still in high school. Clelia and I have been writing friends since grade school.

Thank you, Dutton Foster, for suggesting—between rapids while inner-tubing down the Kinnickinnic River—that I tackle Arthur's point of view, also for your professional critique of the almost-finished manuscript.

I thank my sisters, Patricia Spadavecchia, for her careful critique of character and for holding me to historical accuracy and Caroline Foster, for her sensitive insight and encouragement.

I am grateful for my hardworking editor, Robert Barclay, for his sharp eye for clarity and precise detail which he generously lavished on *Arthur's Room*. With five special-needs adopted children and two novels in print, he is a qualified critic.

Thanks to my industrious publisher, "Beaver" Adams. To Jack Caravela and Brooke Schroeder of Mori Studio. And to my cover artist, Jennifer Bend.

I

July, 1929

The houses lining Crest Avenue were of dark stone or brick in the Victorian-baronial style, immortal monuments to the wealth their builders amassed from lumber, railroading, real estate, or the professional skills and merchandising ventures such a clientele demanded. The city's founding fathers could not imagine mortality for themselves or their neighborhood, and Crest Avenue was zoned "single-family residential in perpetuity."

Unlike their houses, the residents proved mortal. Old Mr. Lufthauser still hobbled to his Daimler on the arm of his uniformed chauffeur, but most of Crest hill had become a neighborhood of widows, many of whom were content to regard the sources of their income as a pleasant mystery. This dwindling population was sparsely reinforced by a new generation, which, with stubborn mid-western conventionality, struggled to maintain a dying lifestyle. Behind the coal soot of aging walls the houses shielded the emotional restraint and social propriety which their ancestral owners had espoused. Yet, within those sarcophagi of tradition, young roots of unrecognized passions quietly swelled.

The sidewalk was empty save for a small dark woman standing across the street from 344 Crest Avenue. She faced a rectangle of smooth gray stone, its pretentious size magnified by the starkness of its architecture. The symmetrical facade's one embellishment was a central door of glass guarded by ornamental grillwork. The very big house was a poignant contrast to the fragility of a four-year-old child.

●

Phyllis's nose was flattened to a small white button against the window glass. From her brother Arthur's room, she looked through a pattern of oak leaves to Crest Avenue where, without touching, old elms arched over the leisurely traffic: square black bodies of Packards, Cadillacs and an occasional Rolls-Royce, the lion's purr of their motors dominating the more abrasive sounds of smaller cars traveling from places Phyllis did not know. No children played on the sidewalk.

A small black-haired woman in a white blouse and skirt of dark blue walked along the far side of the street, arms pressed to her sides and a draw-string bag clutched in one hand. On a cobbled side street across the avenue, a ribby heavy-headed mare pulled a vegetable cart. The woman hurried to the curb as the mare plodded toward her, it's muzzle gray, its ears, wilting sideways. It didn't care about the cars.

Quick with four-year-old excitement, Phyllis used her fist to smear the fog of her breath from the window. "Arthur, Arthur, there's a horse, a real old horse! A horse with a lady watching, a little lady." Phyllis turned a perplexed face to her brother. "She looks different, like she lives somewhere else. Now she's buying some corn and some green leaves."

"Aahh." His mouth was open wide, a deep cave in his face.

Phyllis peered down his throat. "I like to see the little pink jelly bean you got back there," Phyllis said, spying his epiglottis.

The seven-year-old boy sat in a wheel chair, its cane back looming above him. Sunlight shafted into his blinking eyes. "Sun bad?" Phyllis asked. "Miss Bitzer's not here, but I can fix you." Phyllis tugged at the spokes of the wheel; the rim was tall as her eyes. "Better?"

"Aahh," he sighed.

Phyllis returned to her reporting. "Now the lady's taking a piece of paper out of her bag, and she's looking at our house. She's crossing the street. Maybe she's coming here. No..."

Phyllis watched her walk past the stone path to the servants' entrance, away down the block, her string bag heavy with vegetables. "She's gone, so now it's like usual, just houses. When it's just houses it's not so fun any more," Phyllis said. "I don't like just usual." She pushed the curtain aside so that she could see the park across the street where the Indian with his bow and arrow stood on a rock in the middle of a pond where geese spit water into the air. No children played there.

"Now there's nothing. Guess I'll go," Phyllis said. Arthur's wailing voice stabbed after his retreating sister. His head dropped down like a doll with a broken neck. Phyllis skipped and hopped over the dull flowers on the runner down the upstairs hall. She passed her mother's room, the sewing room, the linen closet and the closed door to her father's room. Phyllis knew he was downtown behind the black sign with gold letters:

BAYLIS & DEAN
SPORTING EQUIPMENT
WILDERNESS OUTFITTERS

She opened the oak door to the back hall. The leather of her soles slapped the stairs as she hurried to the kitchen. Maybe Hilda would show her the "wind picture" with the children climbing up to the "big wheel" on top.

Hilda's sturdy pink arm with yellow hairs was cutting bread stale enough to slice thin. Phyllis looked up and asked, "Can I see your sisters and your brother in the wind?"

"Climbing the windmill you mean? No. I'm busy."

Phyllis persisted. "Can I play with them some time?"

"They're too far away. Way up North. Now run along. I've got work to do, all these cucumber sandwiches, and chicken à la king to fix... Your ma. No, *mother*," (her inflection punched the correct word) "is having a luncheon. Those ladies will come any minute. Get upstairs now. Miss Bitzer will help you get dressed." Phyllis poked her way up the stairs.

●

In her dotted-swiss party dress with the lace collar and smocked bodice, Phyllis stood in Arthur's room looking out of the back window. Carl, the gardener, was digging the moist earth around a skinny tree. His five-year-old son, George, stamped his bare foot into the mud.

Phyllis stamped her sandal on the floor, then kicked the wall under the window stinging her big toe. Slowly, drop by drop, angry tears squeezed from her clenched eyelids. "Why can't I be like George?" Sobs choked her words. "Go outside like George, play like him." Phyllis pressed her toes against the straps of her sandals. "But Mother's poem ladies are coming, and I gotta be dressed up and stay clean."

"Aahh," a long sound. Arthur's body contracted in sympathy. But Phyllis regarded him as she would her "Lamby," someone she could talk to with no expectation of response.

With her little finger, callused from four years of sucking, in her mouth, Phyllis studied the leaves of the "mother-tongue plant" on Arthur's windowsill. She looked down the tall sharp spikes to the glistening dirt, then pulled her finger from her mouth with a pop. Steady and deliberate, she plunged her index finger into the dirt, wiggled it, then pulled it out. As she stared at the clinging mud, it told her a way to freedom. She put her mud-wet finger against the collar of her perfectly-laundered dress and pulled it to the hem, then down her legs and over the center strap of her white sandals. Illusions of escape came with knowing she had no cleanliness to preserve, yet she knew Miss Bitzer would return, mad.

"I gotta go," she said, more to herself than to Arthur.

Arthur's pipe-cleaner arms waved from his wide sleeves.

As she ran out of Arthur's room, Phyllis remembered to reach up to the knob and close his door as her mother insisted when she expected company.

Through the thinning crack of the door, just before she spun away to run, she glimpsed Arthur's kicking foot. From his wide mouth, sound roared like zoo-trapped tigers, not *gurr* or *meow* as animals said in the picture books Miss Bitzer read to Phyllis. His anger followed her, roaring and real, as she fled through the long hall and down the long stairways.

She stood at the library entrance behind one of the velvet portieres, trimmed with gold braid, which framed the archway. Her mother's reading voice wafted to her on currents of lilac perfume. The studied diction, which imitated the inflections of the lecturers she listened to on educational radio, was a meaningless drone in Phyllis's ears.

Cautiously she peered through the narrow slit between the wall and the portiere so she could see the six ladies seated in an attentive circle around Deirdre Dean. She almost ran into the room, but then her mother opened the blue book with gold letters and started to talk. Phyllis could not interrupt.

"My favorite poem is yet to come." Her mother's fingers fiddled over the page, but she did not read to the ladies. She closed the book. Phyllis watched her mother's gray eyes shift nervously around the circle of faces. Her oldest friend, Mrs. Patterson, nodded encouragement. Deirdre Dean began, "At times I get..."

Phyllis stepped backward, uneasy with an unfamiliar quaver of emotion shaking her mother's words. That never happened when she read *Mother Goose*. In the pressing silence, Phyllis looked down at her dress, at the thick line she had drawn with the mud-crayon of her finger. Thinking it should feel waxy-smooth, she put the finger in her mouth; her tongue felt the grit of dirt, and the scratch of it foreshadowed punishment.

From the safety of her vantage point, Phyllis stared at the ladies, some white-haired like her mother with snowballs nestled at the naps of their necks, some younger with bobbed hair. Her mother had had white hair forever and ever. It had a wave on each side and a bun in the back.

On a marble-topped table across the room from Phyllis stood a stone Venus, powder-white, looking down at the circle of ladies. Deirdre Dean's face was powdered with the same stone-white. As her nervous fingers flicked from the cameo at her neck to the pages of the book on her lap, a small photograph slipped to the floor. Moving stiffly inside the bones of her corset, she leaned down to pick it up. "Oh my, this poor little picture does prick my memory…." She bent her head over the sepia photograph. "So cracked and faded, just as I am." Polite objections from the ladies were blurred under the trill of Mrs. Dean's self-disparaging laughter. Phyllis knew the photograph. It looked like her old-fashioned doll that was too good to play with.

"What a sweet child! Do tell us who she is." The tall woman to Mrs. Dean's left arched over the picture of a child hidden under a rose-petal dress: long sleeves, all-over puffy with a wide sash. The child's face was framed by a wide bow fanning behind her cork-screw curls.

"Would you believe it? Here I am, a little child. This picture was taken just before my dear sweet mother died."

Phyllis knew the dear-sweet-grandmother on her mother's dresser. Her hair was all piled up, and she was holding a little baby.

Her mother was still talking. "…just like a man, Father was so bumbley about household things. The maids had to manage with the most cursory supervision!

Mrs. Patterson was telling the new people the story Phyllis knew. "…then suddenly her heart gave out; Deirdre's mother died when her little girl was only six."

Phyllis's feet wanted to run, but she knew it still was not time. She watched her mother pulling at the fingers of one hand with the other as Mrs. Patterson talked, to make them longer, Phyllis guessed.

Pleasure and embarrassment twitched across Mrs. Dean's face. She looked down into her lap.

"Fortunately this lovely little girl you're looking at was in the care of a fine nurse. Young though she was when Deirdre's mother died, Miss Bitzer was surrounded by well-trained servants, and Deirdre grew up in a well-regulated home." Mrs. Patterson swept her arm in an arc around the room. "One look at this beautifully run household and you all know how well Deirdre..."

Phyllis started to run....

"Enough, enough!" her mother exclaimed.

Again Phyllis checked her impulse and clutched at the portiere to keep her balance.

"My dear father worked long and hard to acquaint me with the great minds of our culture. Such a time he had! So difficult for me to comprehend!" Mrs. Dean picked up the volume of poetry, then once more put it down in her lap.

"There is one more thing I must tell you. Would you believe it? Our Miss Bitzer, *my* old nurse, all those years with our family, and now she is still loyally serving my dear boy. But Phyllis, she is too much! Much too much for Miss Bitzer to keep track of. Poor old soul; she must be over eighty."

"It is kind of you to keep her on," Jane said.

"How could I do otherwise? We are her family; she has no other. My dear, would you believe it? I was forty-three when my little Phyllis was born, and she would be a handful for a twenty-year-old, so you can see I badly need a young woman who can care for both children."

Can I go out? repeated in Phylis's mind. Pretty soon her feet would fall asleep from standing still so long, but the talk went on and on while she listened for a pause.

"I have found someone, well trained, a registered nurse. I do hope she works out, yet there is something about her..." Mrs. Dean pursed her lips and looked firmly ahead, focusing on the unknown. "This young woman has a most unconventional background. In fact, she is Indian, American Indian." She hastened to add, "but she is refined looking. Her skin is pale, and she never lived on a reservation. She did study in a white nursing school, and she was the only registered nurse who applied."

The heads nodded in agreement, and Mrs. Patterson voiced the pervasive opinion. "All that professional training makes most of them too proud for general work."

"Very true, but this Indian girl found hospital work too technical for her nature. She wanted to work with children, so she was willing to take a job as a general nurse."

Mrs. Dean smoothed her white hair and pushed a hairpin more tightly into the bun at the back of her neck as the photograph finished its circle with scant attention.

"I do admire your tolerance," Mrs. Patterson said.

Phyllis watched the heads and noticed that not all of them were nodding.

"It is so difficult to find the right influences for an impressionable child."

Phyllis wondered if she was the child and *impressionable* meant dirty. She wiggled her muddy sandal so that it almost poked out from behind the portiere.

Her mother was talking—still. "…girls come right off the farm, and they do not know the simplest things about proper procedures, but, as I said, this woman is well educated."

To Phyllis the women looked uncomfortable. Was it "Indians" that were dirty? The woman to Mrs. Dean's right shook a hairpin from her bun, then rushed to change the subject. "My dressmaker story is a humorous illustration of your point. Last week when I went to my seamstress to pick up my dress for the symphony-benefit ball, that little woman poked and stretched at the puckered seams, then tried to explain away her clumsy work, 'It ain't been pressed with no damp cloth yet'."

The general laughter covered Mrs. Dean's comment, "This situation is quite different."

Claudia Patterson returned attention to the purpose of the gathering. "Now do give us your favorite poem, Deirdre."

"Too much talk about me! Now is Emily Dickenson's turn. Listening to 'Understanding the Masters' on public radio has given me a deeper understanding of her poetry. Such a modest person! Yet so lofty, blessed with such Cathedral thoughts. You can almost hear organ music accompanying her poems. Such a fascinating recluse she was!" This time a unity of nodding heads responded.

Mrs. Dean read from pages thin as Bible paper. Her words drifted over and around Phyllis who heard without attending:

> *After great pain a formal feeling comes—*
> *The Nerves sit ceremonious, like Tombs—*
> *The stiff Heart questions was it He, that bore,*
> *And Yesterday or Centuries Before?*
> *This is the hour of Lead—*
> *Remembered, if outlived,*
> *As Freezing persons, recollect the Snow—*
> *First—Chill—then Stupor—then the letting*
> *go—*

A quiver in her mother's voice as she said "letting go" drew Phyllis's attention. She looked into her mother's face, bent low over the book. Phyllis stared at her eyelids fluttering over wet gray eyes. Her mouth was so tight her lips were gone. The mother was gone, the whole mother that Phyllis knew. A grown-up was crying! Upsetting, confusing to see, then feel the familiar strength melt like ice in a fire.

As Mrs. Dean reached down to take a handkerchief from her bag, the portiere stirred, and under it, Phyllis's mud-lined sandals commanded her mother's horrified attention. How could Miss Bitzer be so negligent? Then, tufting from behind the portiere, she saw the bush of her daughter's hair. Mrs. Dean had attempted to tie down those unruly curls, but Phyllis had pulled off the scarf as soon as her mother turned out the bedroom light. In the morning, her hair looked as wild as ever.

"Phyllis! What are you doing?" Her mother's eyes were half hidden behind her handkerchief.

"You don't want me, I'm dirty. So can I go outside and play with George?" The smothered tittering drained strength from Phyllis's voice. "…because I'm dirty already?" She followed her words out from behind the portiere and stood in the wide archway between the library and the front hall. The circle of eyes pierced Phyllis, sending her running across the hall, past the bust of Nofretete on the hall table, past the line of Edwardian chairs too stiff to sit on, to her hiding corner where there was just enough room for her to squeeze between the wall and the grandfather clock. Closed into the corner space, she could hear the pendulum, a metronome of order, swinging with her heart, making it quiet. "All the lady-eyes, they squash me," Phyllis whispered to her clock. Wanting to see the gold sun swinging at the end of its stick, she stepped beyond her protection, hoping she would be safe from the eyes of her mother's friends who were in the hall saying their slow *goodbyes* as they drifted toward the front door.

They saw her. Phyllis shrank from the intrusive compliments: "Phyllis, what beautiful dark eyes you have."…."What a head of curly hair that child has!"…."Such finely chiseled features for a little child, she really does resemble your classic Nofretete." But Phyllis knew, the queen of Egypt wore a crown to squash her hair. Shaking her head, Phyllis put a hand to her curls. As if she expected it to block the words from entering her head, she squeezed her eyes shut, then melted into her corner behind the clock. Safely invisible, she listened to the ticking, not the talk.

A little lady stepped onto Phyllis's garden rug. "Oh my, you do have a lovely carpet, but aren't you afraid of the wear—it being in the entryway?"

"Father brought it to me when he returned from the Orient. In the desert climates the carpets are plagued with blowing sand, so they must be durable. I've heard that only a child's hand can tie such tiny knots."

"Such fine work!" Sarah exclaimed. "As they say, 'the thinner the carpet, the richer the Persian'."

Mrs. Dean shook her head at that ostentatious reference to wealth, something which should be graciously accepted as is the air around us.

"Those rich dark colors! The nomadic tribes saw so much sun! To rest their eyes they liked darkness in the home," Claudia said.

"I like the darkness too; it helps to keep me calm." As

Deirdre spoke, a muffled sound, suggesting a trapped animal in a distant place, drifted down the wide front stairs bringing silence to the slowly departing group.

Claudia Patterson broke the awkward silence. Deirdre, we do understand your need for calm." She put a hand on Mrs. Dean's shoulder as she glanced up the stairs toward the invisible source of the sounds.

"You know I do not want pity. I do not know what I would do without my dear boy."

"You do manage bravely."

Mrs. Dean moved away from the intimate touch of her friend's hand, and Claudia returned to her perusal of the carpet. "Oh look! I'm so excited, I'll be on my knees in a moment!" she exclaimed.

"What is it, dear Claudia?"

"You see this little bird in the corner? The one with the stubby wing?"

"We're all looking." (But Jane's feet took twitching steps toward the front door.)

"That's how you can tell a rug is really genuine. The best ones have irregularities like this stubby wing. You see, only Allah has a right to be perfect."

"But for myself, I cannot help trying." The bell-tinkle of Mrs. Dean's laugh surrounded the exiting ladies. "I am so happy that we could have this time together."

The door finally closed, and Mrs. Dean turned to her daughter. "I thought they would never leave! ...and your new nurse due at any moment."

To Phyllis, *nurse* meant old Miss Bitzer, a wobbly chin her only movement as she sat interminably by Arthur's chair. Nurses read *The Lovable Tales of Janie and Josey and Joe* instead of *Hansel and Gretel* the way Grandmother Dean did. Another one of those nurses in dark dresses would be worse than her mother telling her everything she had to do. But what did *Indian* mean?

"Now behave yourself while I go to lay out clean clothes for you." Mrs. Dean disappeared upstairs, so Phyllis escaped the nasty experience of licking her mother's perfumed handkerchief so that she could wipe the mud from her daughter's face.

Phyllis invented her own outside; she went to the "Persian's garden" in the front hall for her fear-game. She had to walk on tip toe, so carefully, around the Persians' flowers. They must have planted them as Carl planted the gardens around her house, each flower just where her mother told him to. Her heart speeded with her fear: *if I make a bad step...* Her mind, like a fun-house mirror, twisted reality away from her mother's rebukes when she stepped in the flower beds, to scary dragons waiting to spit their fire should she make a misstep. Finally, in the center of the good circle in the center of the rug she sat hugging her legs against her chest, squeezing small enough to fit. Around her the world of dragons threatened, but she was in the safe place where no dragon's teeth could reach.

Phyllis jumped at the harsh ring of the door bell. She ran without caution to the front door before Hilda, in her crackling white uniform, could get ahead of her. Tugging open the inside door took all her strength. The outside door, with its thick glass framed in iron and supported by grillwork twisted into vines with hammered leaves, was too heavy. Phyllis looked through the glass. Under a bunch of iron grapes and level with her eyes was a cage, home to a yellow-headed bird resembling a small cockatiel, but turquoise rather than gray. It raised a scaly foot from its perch, gazed at Phyllis through one glistening eye, then jerked its head to look with the other, making Phyllis laugh. Behind the bird, Phyllis recognized the small woman in a blue skirt and a white blouse. In her broad face, her eyes were bright like black stars in the sky when sunset is still a little red. Phyllis watched the wind blowing "cracks" in her straight black hair so that her ears poked out like rosy sea shells. Her lips moved, speaking without sound.

Phyllis stared until the fun-house of her mind shut down leaving an empty consciousness. As she drifted away from herself, she saw the face turn light around the edges like a cloud when the sun shines from behind it. Her knees wobbled, so she almost fell down; but when she stood straight again, she felt strong; a transfigured little pig still smeared with mud from the "mother tongue" plant in Arthur's room.

Phyllis did something brand new: she opened the door by herself, then told the lady in her loudest voice, "I saw you far away. Out Arthur's room."

"Yes, I was across the street looking at your house, but I didn't see you. And then I got my vegetables from the farmer with the horse, and I took them to a house where I'm staying down below the hill. Thank you for opening that heavy door for me."

Mrs. Dean's heels clicked on the parquet, then were muted by the rug. "Do put down your bags, Edie. Carl will take them to your room. I hope you found us without any trouble."

"Oh yes, I walk by here sometimes. I am staying on Pleasant, below the hill."

"How convenient." Mrs. Dean nodded, then turned to her daughter, "This is your new nurse, Edie."

Phyllis watched Edie smile. "Phyllis and I have met already. She is such a big girl that she opened the door for me." As Mrs. Dean started toward the library, a raucous scream from the bird sent Phyllis running back to her clock.

"Eagle has a loud voice," Edie said, "but he never hurts anyone." With slow steps Phyllis followed the adults into the library. Eagle stayed in his cage in the hall.

Her mother apologized for Phyllis's dirty clothes, then explained Arthur's spastic quadriplegia. "He needs a special person. He is so dear. Such a perfect baby—he was, but difficult. So difficult to feed! He could not suck, you know." Edie nodded. "Then his muscles contracted as his bones grew long. Now he is always tense, his muscles pulling against each other, except in sleep. The spasticity leaves him then, but his muscles can never extend as they should. Emotionally, as I told you in our interview, he is not always steady." Phyllis noticed that her mother did not tell that *not steady* meant he screamed and waved his arms and legs until he fell out of his chair and had to be picked up from the floor.

"It does comfort me to know you are a registered nurse. Choking can be a serious problem for Arthur. He is always in danger of aspirating his food."

"Yes," Edie said softly.

"As I told you in our interview at the employment office, you will be in charge of the children's meals, baths, and clothes." Mrs. Dean continued instructions as she took Edie upstairs to see Phyllis's room, the bathroom, the lists on closet doors specifying when to change the children's clothes, bed times and balanced diets. Phyllis went into her room to get her "blankie" while her mother was explaining to Edie about Arthur's baths and showing her everything in his bathroom.

When Phyllis got back, her mother and Edie were going to see Arthur. They stopped because Miss Bitzer was opening up his pants so he could use his bottle. "This is private time for Arthur and Miss Bitzer," his mother said. "I will introduce you later."

The telephone was ringing as Mrs. Dean said, "Perhaps now you would like to see your room?—but I may have to take this call. I am on the committee for the Children's Hospital benefit treasure sale," she explained. "It demands a great deal of time."

She waited for Hilda to announce, "The telephone is for you, Mrs. Dean."

"I really must go, but Phyllis can show you your room."

Phyllis dropped her blanket and led the way up to the third floor. Carl carried her two suitcases, but Edie carried the birdcage herself. As the cage swung to Edie's firm walk, the bird stretched one turquoise wing and then the other to hold its perch. Then he said clearly, "Open the door."

"Your bird talks a lot better than Arthur."

"But I'll guess that Arthur thinks better," Edie said.

They passed Hilda's room, Miss Bitzer's, then the store room and on to the end of the hall where Carl opened the door to the satin cream of new-painted walls. Edie put the cage on the green wicker table in front of the window that looked over the gardens to the city below and all the way to the silver sliver of the distant Mississippi River.

"Now I need to fill his water dish. Is that the bathroom?" she asked, pointing down the length of the long hall?

Phyllis nodded, then followed Edie with a stream of questions. "What's his name?"

"Eagle."

"Where did Eagle come from?"

"My husband gave him to me for my birthday."

"Did he get him at a pet store?"

Edie turned on the faucet and filled the little dish. "No, he couldn't go to a pet store."

"Why not?"

"Because he was dead."

Phyllis skipped past Edie and the bird. "You mean he was so dead he couldn't go anywhere?"

"That's right. Up to the stars, nowhere we could follow. So he sent Eagle to me."

"That's nice."

"Yes. He told me that he was going to give me a bird for my birthday, but he couldn't go all the way from our farm to the pet store. Then he passed on the day before my birthday." Edie gazed at the stream of water from the faucet as though she were seeing her own tears. "That was the very saddest day in my whole life, and I cried and cried. In the morning when I got up, I cried again."

"You mean like a baby?"

"Yes, but sometimes grown-ups cry too. What happened next—clear as the sun shining through the window, I heard a voice say, *Open*. Then I saw my Eagle sitting on my window sill. I opened the screen. It was warm summer, but suddenly I felt cold."

"Like a snow man?"

"A little like that, but not quite so cold."

"And you let Eagle in?"

"When I opened the screen, Eagle came right to my hand. The people in the hospital where I took care of sick people didn't understand who sent him. They tried to tell me it was someone's pet who flew away." Edie shook her head, and Phyllis could see her ears again. "I didn't believe them. But now we have work to do. Can you help me lift this suit case?"

"It's too big."

"Just try....Get your hands underneath." Phyllis squatted and reached under the suitcase, hugging it against her muddy yellow dress. "That's right, now lift."

Phyllis gazed proudly at the suitcase on the bed. "I didn't know I was so big." She watched Edie open it and put her clothes in piles on the bed. Finally she got to the bottom of the suitcase and took out a brush, some bottles, writing paper and bird food.

"Arthur can't go to a pet shop either. Could he get me a bird if he was dead?"

"I don't think so. Boys seven years old are much too young to die. You and I can both have Eagle." She put bird seed in Phyllis's hand and opened Eagle's cage. Phyllis reached in, and Eagle tickled her palm with his beak as he ate.

When he was through eating, Edie took him out of his cage and held him on his back in the palm of her hand. She showed Phyllis how to stroke his yellow throat and breast. "Very gently now." Phyllis did it just right, and Eagle closed his eyes as if he heard a lullaby.

When Eagle was back in his cage, Edie unwrapped a red cloth around something long and thin.

"What's that? ...Oh, a pointy feather!" Phyllis held out her hand, and Edie showed her how to stroke the "little hairy parts" so that they stuck together.

"It's an eagle's wing feather."

Phyllis shook her head so hard her dark curls swished across her face. "It's too big and black."

"That's because it's from a real eagle, a great big black bird with a white head, not a yellow one like our 'Eagle.' Our little Eagle is a different kind of bird. I named him after his big relative because…" Edie was taking a framed picture out of her suitcase, "our Eagle came from that mystery place where my husband is now." She was standing the man in his mirror frame in the middle of her dresser. He had one hand on the neck of a horse with big hairy feet.

"Oh, your dead man. Mother has a dead picture on her dresser too. It's a grandmother. Mother says 'it's 'a frail-and-lovely-creature-who-died-when-I-was-six.' So she didn't get to have a mother like other little girls. It had the same name as me."

Edie put the feather in its place in back of the man and the horse. She turned around when Arthur's voice came from his room, winding up the stairs and down the hall to her room.

"When he's loud that means he wants something. Maybe you'd like to see him now? He'd be pretty glad to see us. Miss Bitzer's no good for getting things. She belongs sitting down."

"Don't you think we should wait for your mother?"

"I can take you. It's okay." Phyllis paused in the doorway.

"Arthur needs to see Eagle."

"All right. I'll bring him."

Phyllis walked ahead. Her starched skirt swished with the importance of a broom, and she forgot the stripe of mud. "He's steady today."

Edie followed with the birdcage, downstairs. "Please pick up your blanket," she said to Phyllis.

"Can't you do it?"

"No. It's yours to take care of. Please put it in your room."

Edie waited until Phyllis got back, then followed her past Mrs. Dean's bedroom, past all the other doors, to Arthur's dayroom across from his bedroom at the end of the hall. His room was three steps lower than the hall, and Phyllis ran down the ramp that covered them. At the bottom Phyllis stood still and looked from Arthur to Edie who stood at the top looking over the room with windows on three sides. Behind her, pinned to Arthur's bulletin board were the never-changing pictures that

Miss Bitzer cut out of magazines: butterflies, sailboats and children singing in church. On the wall next to the singing children was Arthur's cuckoo clock. The carved vines coiled around the mysterious hole to the cuckoo's nest, camouflaging it with wooden leaves.

Like always, Miss Bitzer sat in the wicker rocking chair with her mouth a little bit open, darning Mr. Dean's new socks so they would last as close to forever as possible. Her dress, as always, was brown and shapeless. Under it she spread out, loose, over her chair. She looked at Edie with her eyes, but her face stayed the way it always was. "You gotta talk loud or she can't hear you," Phyllis said.

"Thank you. I will." In a loud voice she said, "I'm Edie Markson."

Miss Bitzer nodded slowly.

"And you're Miss Bitzer?"

Miss Bitzer nodded again. "I'm Arthur's nurse," she said in her slow, scratchy way.

Arthur's back was to the windows, so he saw Edie coming, saw her put the bird-cage on the floor. She was looking right at him. But her face was not surprised.

Like a thin rubber doll, old and partly melted, Arthur was bent down in his deep cushion. Hair straggled over his ears as the barber would come to cut it only after much persuasion. His clothes, as always, were clean, kept that way by a terrycloth bib tied around his neck to catch the perpetual river of saliva running down his chin. His blue shirt and favorite maroon sweater hung from his thin shoulders with an empty look as if still on a hanger. Waving out of control, Arthur's arms and legs were like his voice, equally severed from his brain. Like the wrist bones that protruded from his sleeves, the bones of his face were sharp under his stretched skin. As he smiled at Edie, it stretched even farther back from the gaping hole of his mouth.

When Phyllis looked at Edie, she was smiling back at Arthur. There was something behind it unfamiliar to Phyllis, unaccustomed as she was to seeing emotion expressed so openly.

Perhaps Edie saw Arthur in that strange way Phyllis had seen Edie for the first time: with light shining around his unrevealing features. All the usual signals one human gives another were voided by Arthur's lack of control. His fist was friendly, his shaking head meant neither *yes* nor *no*. His yawning mouth could mean anger or a laugh.

"This is the bird lady," Phyllis announced to Authur.

Arthur made his noise, his arm jerked to the side. Edie came down the ramp and took his fist in her two hands. Her bird called out a sharp greeting, a hospitable "Open the door."

Arthur's head bobbed with excitement, and he kicked off one of his socks. Phyllis dropped to all fours to pick it up. Then, avoiding a kick, she grabbed the leg, scissored and wooden, emerging from navy shorts. She explained, "Arthur can't wear shoes because he's got twisted feet, so Miss Bitzer knits him socks round and round without any heels."

"Do you need help getting that sock on?" Miss Bitzer asked in a voice that was settled deep in the rocking chair with the rest of her.

Phyllis got the sock on after a couple of tries.

"Now would you like to bring Eagle's cage close to Arthur?" Phyllis bumped it with her knees at every step.

Arthur roared out his laughter and waved his arms spreading contagious joy. The clock's cuckoo burst out of his house, and Eagle called, "Open the door." Even Miss Bitzer moved her elbows just slightly.

As suddenly as it began, all laughing stopped except for Arthur's final gasps. When Phyllis looked to the top of the ramp, there stood her mother. Her forehead was wrinkled with confusion, then her words smoothed it. "This noise really does seem uncalled for. I am concerned for Arthur. He is so frail, and we must keep him from becoming overly excited, the tension you know." She surveyed the quiet room, smiled and nodded. "Now I must finish my telephone conversation. Edie, I would like to speak to you after you take your bird back to your room." She walked up the ramp, her toes pointed out in a neat *V*.

Nothing to answer. Mrs. Dean had gone before Arthur's voice ran down. Even silence was something he could not come to quickly. Edie picked up the birdcage and walked up the ramp. When they looked back at Arthur, his cheeks were as wet as his chin. Tears. He was quiet, but, by the time they walked down the hall, the screaming had started.

Edie stopped so quickly the cage banged against the wall. In a plugged voice she asked, "Shouldn't we go back?"

"He's not steady, but he stops pretty soon when he falls out of his chair. We're supposed to wait."

Phyllis's hand reached up to Edie's. For the second time that day she saw a grown-up weep. Edie stood still and blew her nose. "I'm going back," she said.

Phyllis followed her and stood at the top of the ramp. Arthur was on the floor in front of his chair, like a pile of clothes in the laundry room under the clothes chute. Phyllis watched Edie unfold his arms from under him, put her hands under his shoulders and lift him. Before she seated him into his chair, he was straight up against her, and she put her arms all the way around him and hugged him for a long time. Arthur was making sounds that choked in his throat, and Edie's voice was too soft to hear.

She helped him sit down, then stood beside him. Her hands floated over his shoulders, his face and his neck. The sound in Arthur's throat gentled until it became soft as a cat's purr while Edie talked to him. "Don't try. Don't try anything. Let the fear float away."

Arthur felt the slip of her fingers up from his eyes across his forehead. He felt the slide of her hands on his temples, down his cheeks to his throat. He tried to feel it better, push through the clutch of fear. The shell around him tightened, tightened until it cracked. For a moment, only a moment, his mind went away, releasing the fear and the struggle. His muscles were soft as sleep.

●

Sitting on the edge of Phyllis's spool bed as the morning sun sneaked around the window shades, Edie listened to the child's dream world. "I was like Eagle or an angel, like part of the sky. But now I'm just a popped balloon."

"You'll fly again. Even birds come down sometimes." Edie went to raise the shades, then took Phyllis to the window and pointed to the sun-touched dew. "See the light fly up from the ground?"

"No. That's dew. It can't get up, and it's crying."

"The sun will shine the tears away like a great warm handkerchief, then the dry grass will be waiting for your feet, feet in *new shoes*."

"New shoes!?" Phyllis quickly forgot her dream.

Goslings were the shoes everybody on the hill got for their young children. They were of soft creamy leather and hand stitched by four bearded brothers from Germany, all under five feet tall. The shoes resembled moccasins, a modicum of comfort Phyllis's mother provided for her daughter.

On this "new shoes day" Phyllis's mother was busy with workmen who were to install glass panels in the cabinet doors of the linen closet. "Even with labels on the doors the laundress makes mistakes. Once this is done, I'll be able to check at a glance," Mrs. Dean told Edie who heard without comment. "As you can see, I am completely involved, so Carl will drive you." She was nervously tapping the floor with a yardstick. "The shoes have been ordered, and the men are meticulous about fit, so all you will have to do is see that there is growing space at the toe, then sign the charge."

Phyllis was impatiently waiting by the door when Carl parked the black Cadillac in the driveway beside the house. Phyllis tumbled into the car so quickly that she tripped over the jump seat and landed headfirst on the gray plush carpet. Edie helped her up, and they were on their way. Carl's son, George, sat in the front seat beside his father. With the wonder of a traveler among foreigners, Phyllis watched the back of his round blond head constantly turning, alert to the speeding action around him. She followed his pointing hand as he asked, "What's 'at?"

Carl answered in his rhythmic Scandinavian accent with the model and year of a passing car, or explained what a workman with a jackhammer was doing.

Not satisfied with Carl's prosaic answers, Phyllis asked Edie, "But really why?" and Edie turned the concrete "smoke" from the jackhammer into the breath of a bull buffalo buried under the street and steaming from his prison. Phyllis added walls made of new shoes from trampled children.

"But the Buffalo told them they could live again if they would make him free. So they did, and the buffalo made them his relatives, and they all lived on a big prairie."

On the way home Phyllis held the toy Edie bought for Arthur, a brown bear. She moved her fingers in the soft fur and wiggled her toes in the growing space her new shoes provided.

"Your new shoes are soft like the moccasins my people used to wear."

Phyllis's eyes were wide with admiration. "You mean Indian people?"

"Indians!" George exclaimed waving an imaginary gun. "Bang! Bang! Bang! Shoot 'em dead."

"You listen to too many cowboy shows. Be careful," Carl said. "There's lots of good Indians, and if you do bad, they'll sneak up with their bows and arrows, and you'll never know what hit you. Right Edie?"

"Or they'll sneak up behind you so quietly you'll never hear a thing and then grab the gun out of your hands."

George twisted his head to look over the seat. "Like the Indian in the park."

His father laughed, "For sure he'll wear more clothes."

Then Edie said, "I never knew Indians very well, not even my parents for long. I went away to school when I was eight years old. After that I worked for a nice lady named Mrs. Bunn. I helped her take care of her mother, and she helped me go to nursing school. Without her, I couldn't have afforded it."

Phyllis studied her new shoes. "But they should have beads like real moccasins." Phyllis poked the bead-eyes of the bear. "Can I take Arthur's bear to bed, just for tonight?"

"No. It belongs to Arthur."

"Just one night," she pleaded.

"No. Arthur will like to take his own bear to bed. You have Lamby."

Disappointed resignation silenced her for the rest of the way home, but Edie entrusted her to present the bear to Arthur. Clutching it to her breast, Phyllis ran down the ramp and put the bear on his lap. His head shook faster than usual as Edie helped him lock his fingers around its neck.

Phyllis worked at hopping, skipping and jumping until supper time.

She finished her supper in the kitchen and started up the front stairs with Edie when the tall clock struck. The front door opened and slammed behind Mr. Dean.

"Let's go see your father," Edie said, turning to go back down the stairs.

The glass covering the long pendulum of the clock was still vibrating as the last clang of seven faded. Mr. Dean was walking across the hall to the living-room. His long legs swung in an even way, like pendulums. He took the album of "Beethoven's Fifth Symphony" from the shelf, wound the Victrola and put on a record. Phyllis started at the sudden sound. Her father unclipped a pencil from his coat pocket, sat down at his corner desk and bent over the cross-word puzzle on the last page of his paper.

Edie stood beside Phyllis in the wide archway between the front hall and the living room. "Now would be a good time to show him your new shoes."

"No, I can't. Not when he's playing cross puzzles. Mother says not to disturb him. You know how fathers are. They're tired, and they like to play puzzles."

"But they like to see new shoes too, and they like their little girls to talk to them."

Phyllis shook her head. "Not mine. Mother said. Not fathers that are hard of hearing from the war. He likes loud. Mother says it's a strain to listen to little girls, and fathers don't like strains."

"You have a nice loud voice, but, if you'd rather not talk, just show him your new shoes."

"If you want me to." Phyllis slid one foot back and forth over the rug. She started, then stopped. "You'll wait right here till I get back?"

"I'll wait."

The thundercloud of music was in front of her. It wrapped her up. Phyllis put her hands over her ears, but then walked on tiptoes so that she needed to spread her arms like wings to hold her balance. She stopped beside his chair, her eyes level with a grape vine carved in the arm. Her father was studying the puzzle in front of him. Phyllis raised one leg up until she could touch her shoe, then hold it and lift it to the seat of her father's chair. The shoe brushed his thigh.

His breath squeezed out of him like air from the fireplace bellows, then he jerked his chair back, tipping her to the floor. She fell on her side, hitting her head against the leg of the desk. Phyllis didn't hit hard, but when she looked up she saw her father standing above her, then leaning down. He put his face close to hers, almost touching. She gasped, feeling as much surprise as though the soldier in the entry hall had come down out of his frame. His mouth was straight as his sword; but her father's mouth smiled, showing Phyllis a line of white teeth with a space between the two in the middle. "My little mouse was so quiet I didn't hear her coming. You surprised me so I jumped. Up, up to Daddy's lap!" His big hands wrapped around his daughter's waist lifting her to the rough cloth of his trousers. "It isn't such a bad bump now, is it?"

Phyllis's fear drained away, and she put her foot into her hand and lifted the shoe for her father to see.

"Well now, that's a fine looking shoe. Did you get that today?"

Phyllis nodded, then slid off her father's lap and darted back to Edie, eager to tell her. "He was glad! He was really glad!"

"Of course he was. And now it's time for bed."

But Phyllis didn't follow Edie right away, not before she ran back to her father and kissed him on the cheek. He stood up and followed her as she ran to Edie and caught up with her in the hall. "I like his scratchy face."

Phyllis saw Edie smile at her father. He rubbed his whiskery chin and smiled back. "Good night, you two," he said.

"Good night, Mr. Dean." Edie took Phyllis's hand. "Now it's time to say *good night* to Arthur and Eagle."

Miss Bitzer had gone to her room, so Edie stayed with Arthur, and Phyllis brushed her teeth all by herself. Then Edie tucked her in, and hugged her good night after they both blessed all their animal relatives, Lamby and Arthur's bear too.

From far away in her bed Phyllis could hear the symphony ending and ending and ending with crashes like Arthur's mad.

December, 1930

Phyllis had celebrated her fifth birthday on March twenty seventh, and Arthur's eighth birthday would be coming soon on January ninth.

During the day Eagle's cage was nearly always on the table by Arthur's chair. Carefully wrapping his feet around his perch, he sidestepped from one end of his cage to the other and climbed the bars with feet as prehensile as fingers. His curved beak was as useful as another hand. Miss Bitzer just looked at the snow. After a time she said, "Phyllis, you stay with Arthur now. I'm going for my hour off." With her hands on the arms of the rocker, she pushed herself out of the chair and stomped up the ramp. Above her wide seat, she tapered like a spruce tree to the tight gray bun at the back of her neck.

Phyllis listened to Eagle's squawks punctuated by occasional words. "Eagle talks like you, and I have to guess, an... Now he says, 'Open, open, open the...'" Then Phyllis looked at Arthur's mouth shaped like a wide "Door."

"Did you say *door*?"

Arthur was moving his arms hard, and his legs kicked hard too. Then he hit the cage with his fist. His eyes were laughing, and, in their brilliance, Phyllis sensed an alluring *bad*. "Mother says birds have 'unsanitary habits',," she said, her hands hesitating on the cage door—well, okay."

Flight feathers made a windy snap. With excitement at the energy they had released, Phyllis reached to hold Arthur's arm. "We did it, both of us!" Arthur rolled his head to watch, and Phyllis jumped to follow. "He's so strong up there!" The bird dropped to Arthur's head. He laughed, arms and legs reached, and Eagle flew to Phyllis's hair, spreading excitement, too much for the room to hold.

"We mustn't ever catch him. He's having too much fun." The bird sat on Arthur's hand. They looked at each other, Arthur and Eagle. "Edie too! She's in my room, but she wants to see," Phyllis shouted back as she ran.

Edie was rolling up socks and putting them in rows in Phyllis's top drawer, all the whites together and then the other colors in the second row. The right way.

"Come see Eagle."

"When I finish putting away the laundry." Her busy voice surprised Phyllis who expected to find Edie always centered on her whenever Arthur didn't need her. Now Edie seemed away in her own life, perhaps struggling to be companion to the children, Mrs. Dean's employee, and through it all herself. "Ummm," was all Edie said.

Phyllis sat on the rug, got up, then jumped on the bed.

Edie's hands stopped moving, but she did not attend to Phyllis's misbehavior, and Phyllis stopped jumping to watch as Edie looked through the window at the winter sky barred by the branches of an old oak. Phyllis watched her face, as still as the gray sky and the frozen oak. To Phyllis, accustomed as she was to Edie's animated expression, the face she knew was almost gone. Then, as though she had been called, Edie ran to Arthur.

Eagle was not in his cage. Arthur was quiet; tear tracks shined his cheeks. Phyllis followed his focus toward the window, then to the floor. Eagle lay with his yellow head between his feet. Phyllis picked him up, cradled him on his back in her left hand and stroked his throat feathers gently as she had learned from Edie, but he didn't close his eyes. Next she held him up, but his head fell limp. His eyes stayed open, but they didn't shine. She shook him hopefully. One turquoise wing feather drifted to the floor.

"You know you shouldn't have..." But then Edie took Phyllis in her arms and pressed her tight, almost too tight. Phyllis felt Edie's soft body with the strength of big bones supporting them both.

When her sobbing came, it was hard not to squeeze the bird. "Why did Eagle get killed?"

Phyllis and Edie turned to Arthur, followed his spiraling look, round and round until his focus came to rest on the clean window, the glass invisible except for one small downy feather clinging to its center.

Phyllis buried her head against Edie's skirt. "I'm afraid, afraid my mind will keep it in my head."

"Eagle will be happy with the mystery in the stars. We'll remember him, but we'll find new things to love."

"Will your daddy give us another bird?"

"My husband? No, I don't believe he will."

Edie took the warm bird from Phyllis's hand. She wrapped it in one of Arthur's large handkerchiefs. Her body was quivering, and Phyllis knew they were feeling the same about Eagle. She hugged Edie's legs as hard as she could.

Edie put his bear on Arthur's lap and wrapped his fingers around it where the fur was matted. His grip locked.

September, 1931

Phyllis and Arthur watched the summer wearing out and changing into fall. Edie had been their heart-mother for nearly half of Phyllis's life, so long that her real mother became a fairy-tale stepmother.

Edie's day off gave Phyllis a premonition of emptiness to come. She wandered up to Edie's room which smelled of soap and powder, not the heavy flower imitation that wafted from her mother's room. Phyllis stared at the bird cage and let her imagination form a memory of Eagle, but the bird smell was missing in the clean and empty cage. She went to "Edie's dead man," looked back and forth from his thin face under the Eagle feather to her own reflection in the mirror frame. The feather started to move the way it did when the picture talked to Edie. "What are you saying?... Is it a secret?... You talk to Edie. Why don't you talk to me?" Phyllis felt anger clouding around her.

The house had become strange, full of voices behind closed doors and footsteps that chopped. In the morning she heard her mother say into the telephone, "I simply cannot teach her the mental discipline of rationality; she is telling our children fantastic *lies*, and Phyllis believes everything she says. How can the child ever become a serious, rational adult?" Phyllis had run away from the telephone. But when she went down into the kitchen, Miss Bitzer was there telling Hilda that "Edie is a witch" because she knows everything Arthur says.

Phyllis turned her attention back to the picture on the dresser. "I know you can talk," she said. She was sure he nodded his head and even smiled at her.

"Phyllis..." Hilda's voice from down stairs sounded angry; Phyllis was late for lunch. Her mother was already sitting down with the empty white damask spreading out beyond the two set places. Everything was quiet. "Phyllis, you are late. Where have you been?"

Her mother's censure made her feel small, and she spoke softly. "I was talking to Edie's father."

"Please repeat in your grown-up voice."

"Talking to Edie's Mr. Markson," she corrected.

"What do you mean, Child?"

"Up in Edie's room, the picture on her dresser. With his big horse. They all lived on the farm, and then they had to sell it. Because he was dead."

"You went up to Edie's room?"

"She lets me."

"The third floor belongs to the maids, and you are not to go into their rooms without being invited. Never when they are out."

"I forgot. But he didn't answer me, so it's all right?"

"Of course he did not answer. Pictures do not talk."

"Edie talks to him all the time. He's always good. He keeps his promises. So he gave Eagle to Edie for her birthday, like he said. Even after he was dead."

"Dear Child, Dear Child! Such foolishness! A fairytale in a book is one thing, but pretending all this nonsense about pictures talking is real, that is something completely different."

Phyllis felt the words wash around her and spill inside, turning food bad: mashed potatoes stuck up dry and cold next to wrinkled peas, little pieces of meat, cut up, but dry and tough. Only the floating island, with its peak of meringue topping the golden custard, looked good; but the tempting desert sat just beyond the reach of her short arms. She pushed her fork at the meat, a lump of gravy slipped off the plate and fell on her dress. She rubbed it with her napkin.

Hilda was going around the table sweeping crumbs into a silver tray with a stiff pad. Phyllis could hear the brush of her starched uniform as her pink arms moved mechanically. The one with the crumb pad snapped like a whip. Her eyes couldn't look "spooky" because her face puffed too tightly around them. She swished behind the Japanese screen that hid the swinging door to the kitchen. The sound of the swinging became softer and softer as the door waved itself still.

Mrs. Dean left the table, and Phyllis heard her clinking in the silver closet, counting butter knives. They were so small that they could be thrown out in the garbage when the plates were scraped. She peered around the mahogany door. "Phyllis, Dear Child, I do so want you to eat your good lunch."

"I'm not hungry." She poked her fork into the potatoes and slowly twisted it. "Edie lets me eat floating island."

Her mother's head protruded from the closet. "You mean she allows you to eat desert before you have finished your meat and potatoes and vegetables?"

How to help Edie? If she made herself eat? She twisted her fork into the pile of cold "furry" white. She closed her eyes and opened her mouth as she lifted her fork, then took the bite. She tried to swallow; the fur stuck in her throat. Her stomach rebelled. She leaned over her plate as the bile of everything she hated spilled from her mouth, and she tasted all the bitter words she couldn't speak.

Her mother didn't see.

She ran to the lavatory under the stairs. She stood on the stepping stool and watched the clean water run into the marble sink. She cleaned her mouth, then let the water run down her chin as Arthur did before Edie taught him how to swallow all the time, not only food.

●

Fall winds were blowing away the summer, and Phyllis felt the chill of fear. Mourning doves cooed in the ivy that crept up the stone of the house. Their voices were hurried, short time for winter packing. Inside the house Edie's gaze was veiled, looking beyond Phyllis as if she were not there. Mrs. Dean's face was like the Easter card Miss Bitzer got for Arthur, a sad angel with lavender and lilies behind it.

Phyllis heard pieces of talk, big, heavy words: "Reasonable logic...dignity...respect and reverence...parental prerogatives."

Phyllis stopped in the hall outside her father's bedroom door when she heard her mother talking to him. "I have no control over her whatsoever." Phyllis felt her mother's censure a blow at her. But, as the voice continued she realized, unbelievably, *It's Edie!* "....She listens politely," her mother said, "then does with the children exactly what she chooses. Outside with bare feet, clothes torn and dirty when she comes back in, vegetables left on Phyllis's plate unfinished. I could go on and on."

"Don't. I told you what I think—not that I expect it to make any difference."

"Not merely her physical care. That woman is teaching pagan…"

Her father slammed the door, and the doorframe shivered.

Phyllis felt little. She went to the front hall to her Persian rug and sat in the center of the foreign garden. But now she had grown too big to squash into the safe circle. Her toes touched the blue flower, and the dragons were near enough to bite.

The door to the back hall opened. Mrs. Dean was talking. "All we mortal parents can do is trust that we are guided to make the correct decisions, but…" she searched her memory for appropriate words, then recited, 'To know the seed, that is divine indeed'."

Edie's voice was soft as baby moss, too faint to hear.

●

Two days later Phyllis was stringing wooden beads on a long shoelace. *Baby toy*—She shook the beads rolling to the floor. The smell of fresh-baked cookies wafted into her room luring her down to the kitchen. Arthur's favorite cookies sat cooling on the counter: bears with chocolate fur.

Holding a cookie, Phyllis passed the stove, went to the back hall that separated the kitchen from the maids' dining room. In the hall she stopped abruptly without taking another bite. Edie's two suitcases and the empty bird cage were standing against the wall by the door. Through the window she saw big Carl come up the back steps. Phyllis was clamped between the life she knew and the threat of a new one she refused to believe as she watched Carl pick up the small suitcase and put it under his arm, then grip the big one in his hand. He opened the door, taking Edie's suitcases away.

Phyllis heard her mother's voice, then Edie's. Not the words, only the tone. She ducked into the maids' dining room. She clutched the door frame, like a raft to hold her above waves of fear that started in her stomach, swelled inside and washed at her throat and up to her forehead.

The first clear words were her mother's. "I have tried to think of a happier solution, but I am afraid this is the best way. It is the parent's duty to protect and train the minds of their children as they think best. Please try to understand. Of course we shall miss you. In many ways you have been such a treasure."

"Where's Phyllis?" like a stranger using Edie's voice, not knowing how. "I want to say good-bye to her."

"I thought it would be best not to. She is so devoted to you. The parting would be too difficult for her. I shall break it to her gently."

"No, I..." Phyllis heard her say it loud. She sprang from her hiding place and buried her face in Edie's coat, her arms holding on, keeping Edie. Cookie crumbs rubbed into her coat and sifted to the floor.

"Phyllis, my darling, I'll see you again. Believe me, I'll see you again."

"When?"

"I can't tell you that now, but you have Arthur."

"But he can't do things...." Phyllis sobbed.

"Stop. Please. I need to tell you something." Phyllis held back her tears and listened. "Take care of Arthur, teach him and let him teach you."

Edie pried Phyllis's arms loose, and suddenly she was gone.

Phyllis ran from her mother, stumbled into the front hall and clawed at the front door trying to get out, but it was bolted, and she was too upset to turn the lock. She fell to the floor and kicked at the flowers in the rug with her heels.

Phyllis sobbed herself into exhaustion, then lay still. Arthur's cries twisted down the stairs. Breathing deeply she drew in those cries and made them her own.

Arthur was on the floor, his head caught on the footrest of his chair and his body tightened to angles like crumpled paper. Air cooled his body where, only a few moments before, Edie's arms had held him against her warmth, and her voice had soothed him. Finally his cavern of loss was empty, even of sobs; then he could hear, for the first time, Edie's parting words. "Your oak tree is strong. He'll take care of you."

Through his open window, oak leaves flickered to him. They whispered *sshh*, and Arthur heard a friend speak comfort. He answered, "Aahh," then closed his eyes. Knotty arms reached around him, held him in strength and eased his head off the footrest to lower it onto the rug. When he opened his eyes, the tree was outside, the same as always.

Behind the closed door of her room, Mrs. Dean stretched stiffly on her rose-bud chaise. Her righteous strength was melting fast, dissolved in the sounds of her children's pain. But she did not stir from her room. She let their cries pierce her, every desperate note a paralyzing needle drugging her to immobility.

Her children were hers again, but farther removed than they had ever been.

II

May, 1934

The cloudy morning darkened the foliage outside Arthur's window, but his thoughts felt the new life of spring.

He tried to hold his head still while his eyes followed the birds as fast as they flew, in and out of sight beyond his window frame. Pieces of stories hunting a home blew into his head and played there. He would feed marshmallows to the dirty gray bird until she floated up and turned into a white cloud. Then she would say pictures to him in cloud-talk. The blue-black one would melt into rain, and a black dog would drink the bird-water until he was backwards rain and fell up into the sky; then he would bark thunder. Arthur wanted to tell the cuckoo bird in his clock, but he wouldn't come out. There was no person to tell and no words to say it even if someone were there. Arthur's mind stopped playing.

Too many images talked at once. Their voices thundered in his mind, then they started to die, even rot like that mouse that died in his wall in the winter. The dead pictures were in a trap without any food, and they hurt his head. *I want Phyllis.* If she said his thoughts, his ears would hear clear sounds. Edie could do that, but Arthur's new thoughts had left her a shadow-memory from long ago. *I want Phyllis.* "Aah!"

The mad feeling came with claws inside of him. *I want Phyllis.* The mad grew big, stronger and stronger. It held his muscles tight until they burst; then he fell, hard, out of his chair. Like his oak tree, his bones were his branches, and he liked to hear them hitting the floor. The sound was strong, in spite of the cushioning rug Miss Bitzer put under his chair. He felt bigger when he hurt in new places.

He called loud enough to fill the whole house. *I want Phyllis.* "Aah!" But Miss Bitzer heard all wrong. She brought his bottle instead, covered by a white cloth. She called Phyllis to help lift him back into his chair.

"My old back," she said. "This work is much too hard for me."

"Eeh—"

"My old ears can't hear you right."

"Eeh—" Arthur repeated, louder.

But Miss Bitzer did the wrong thing again. She sent Phyllis away. "Later, Dear. This is private time."

Arthur's arms waved but refused to point at Phyllis. "Waa—" Miss Bitzer did not listen. She took the cloth off his bottle and got his pants ready, but he had only a little drip. Then she was mad. She said, "Why did you call me?"

Phyllis was in the hall. She ran ahead of Miss Bitzer when she went to the bathroom with the "milk bottle" decorously hidden under the large napkin.

Arthur watched Phyllis's back until Miss Bitzer's big bulk got in the way. But she didn't come back. Waiting for Phyllis. Time would not move. Steps, but it was his mother coming. He wanted to tell her. *I am twelve. I want to do things. I want to go out.* She wouldn't understand.

Mrs. Dean listened with ignorance born of denial and heard through her fear of knowing her son. Her hand ruffled his hair. With his words a mystery to her, she laughed as loving mothers laugh at their babies' warbles, then left him with an affectionate pat on his arm, her incomprehension smoothing her face with ignorant serenity.

Arthur's turmoil continued unnoticed.

He, the quiet center, alone except for a buzzing fly, the only thing in the room that was not quiet. His eyes followed the flight, round and round in widening circles until the electric-blue body hit the window glass. The little thud jarred Arthur's awareness of the dull ache in his chest, always with him, perhaps caused by the clamp of his ribs around his lungs, by his inability to lift his chest to make room for breath.

He watched the door. A long time. Then Phyllis came carrying paper and colored pencils. "Hello," she said.

"Hh—oo," he said. Glad to see her—did she know? Tell Phyllis about the fly with hair legs, cellophane wings? Feeling little like only a fly.

Arthur wordlessly sensed without the clarity expression gives. His regulated surroundings made his wishes meaningless, turned his ideas into his mother's until his real thoughts became empty wind carrying nothing beyond himself. His caretakers protected him from their own embarrassment transforming his desires to figments of their imagination: he need never feel the shame of public exposure to a stranger's eyes or a stranger's ears. The house around Arthur was a castle staffed to fill his needs as others perceived them. His, the influence of a king, the power of a fly.

"Eeea—" He stopped trying as though his crippled words crippled his thoughts.

"I'm trying to draw a garden," Phyllis said, "but I can't get it right. I can just see it, with butterflies. But it's like the butterflies are in a jar, and they can't fly. You can't get your words out, and I can't get my butterflies out." Phyllis looked up from Arthur's open mouth and watched his eyes, steady, brown, like hers, flecked with gold. They seemed so clear she believed she could see the thoughts inside. They focused on the fly. The straining muscles of his neck tightened, slowly pushing the heavy voice toward meaning, "—open—please."

Not Arthur's spoken words, but a changed level of hearing led Phyllis to the window. She opened it, then the screen. As the buzzing insect flew away, the muscles of her legs twitched with desire to follow.

A track of saliva, like a tear, coursed down Arthur's chin. His thoughts divided into separate balls, like shocked mercury, between the past and present. Edie's hands came out of his memory; he could feel them soothing his throat, stroking his skin, telling him he could swallow. Now it was Phyllis telling him his words could act. His thoughts gained power, came together in a single silver bubble. "It's—nice—to—watch—the—fly—go—free."

Phyllis looked through her brother's face to focus on his inarticulate vowel sounds. She heard each word, saw each one a picture from his eyes. She translated his own words, fast and clear.

He heard a miracle. *Like Phyllis. I can talk.*

Her knuckles turned white as she gripped the seat of her chair, holding herself down. She restrained herself from going to Arthur to kiss the hollow of his cheek.

Already her mother's pattern of reserve was reaching out to hold Phyllis, and she heard her mother's words: *control yourself.*

Standing...going.... She heard Arthur speak again. "Don't—go—away—Please don't...."

She could feel her heart beating, loving Arthur. But her legs were twitching, and she had to run up the ramp, away from too much feeling.

●

Alone in her room, Phyllis crumpled her old unfinished garden, threw it into the wastebasket.

New concepts swelled against the boundaries of her old world, the one made by grown-ups to mold her thoughts in the image of theirs. She needed a new space to hold this new secret: *No one else knows—Arthur can talk.*

Phyllis searched beyond the rose and white of her room, beyond the gray stone of her house; the streak of a blue jay claimed her floating gaze. It lit on a dead branch, so close to the window, printing her mind with each feather from tail to crest. It flew, then called back in a voice that shivered Phyllis's heart. *Arthur needs that bird.* She ran to her table, her restless fingers snatched paper and a pencil. Beak first, open for the song, left eye, head, body, then strong wings with each feather separate, tight with care.

Finished from claws to crown, yet needing something more...

Loud, she heard her mother's voice. "Phyllis Dean! How many times do I have to call you!" *Mother mustn't see.* Quick, under the table. When the door opened, her bird was gone.

"You must come quickly when I call. Grown-ups have important things to do."

●

When night came, Phyllis put her bird on the table by her bed so that she could reach into the darkness and stroke the paper. Her fingers slowed, ready for sleep, and she pulled them back to the warmth of her covers. She twisted at the corner of the little pillow that had been hers for as long as memory, twisted until she felt a stab through the aging linen. She found a quill and pulled out a feather, brushed the down across her lips. She ripped the worn case and filled her hands with feathers. She swung her legs to the floor. In the day-bright hole the lamp made in the dark, she imagined a bird, all white.

With feathers and glue she transformed her common jay into a fluffy angel bird.

One foot was already on her bed when, with an abrupt turn, she ran into the dark, to her doll dresser. She pulled open a drawer, reached down and back under soft cloth. Her hand clutched an envelope, crumpled and torn. Inside was a turquoise feather, not soft and fluffy but strong to lift a bird high.

Late, she crawled back into bed.

Morning footsteps clicked against her ears. She snatched her picture from the bedside table and slipped it under the bed before her mother came into the room.

"What! Still in bed on this lovely morning? Get up quickly now. You're letting the day's best hours slip away." Phyllis watched her mother sit the doll against the cushion on the window seat, then smooth the lavender silk of its dress. "Now she's all ready for the day." Her mother's bright look darkened. "Feathers everywhere!" she exclaimed.

With growing fear Phyllis watched the spiraling drift of a feather as she moved in her bed.

Phyllis saw her mother's eyes fix on the little pillow. Her bustling manner changed as she sat down on the edge of Phyllis's bed, picked up the limp pillow and held it against her cheek. Her face turned sad. "I see now. It really is worn out."

"Can Miss Bitzer fix it?"

"I am afraid the material is just too thin." She stroked her daughter's hair without any attempt to smooth the tight curls. "Did you know that pillow was once mine? My dear mother made it for me when I was a little child, younger than you. See her delicate stitches?—that little lamb with a daisy in its mouth?"

"Tiny, tiny," Phyllis responded. Her mother put her arms around her, but Phyllis wiggled uncomfortably feeling nine-years-old, too big for her mother's cuddling. Deirdre Dean looked away from her daughter to the feathers strewn over the rug.

The white drift partially covered an envelope. She picked it up and examined it carefully. "Edie!" she exclaimed, then read aloud, '*Until I see you again—Love Edie.*' How strange. The past suddenly with us again. You were only six years old. …that summer…." she murmured nostalgically, then shook her head as though to remove a confusion of emotion. "But those were good times." Her voice rose in a question as though puzzled by her feelings. Mrs. Dean reached into the envelope, empty. "I wish I knew what it had held."

She was in the hall beyond Phyllis's hearing as she muttered, "but she was alienating my children, stealing their minds and their love."

●

Phyllis did not share her mother's surprise. Edie had often returned to visit with big Carl and his plump wife, Ilie. Hilda hovered in the background and looked at them sideways as they sat around the table in the maids' dining room. Phyllis enjoyed the sweet crunch of a cookie as the grownups reminisced over their coffee. Of course Edie would always go upstairs to see Arthur. Her last visit had been nearly a year ago. Like a doe at weaning time pushing her fawns away, Edie had gradually separated from the children. Phyllis treasured the little animals Edie had carved out of ivory soap, a gift slight enough to escape Mrs. Dean's notice, as was the turquoise feather. Phyllis had not been sworn to secrecy, but her instincts advised silence. Now Eagle's feather was hidden again, this time as part of Phyllis's art, an extension of herself. She slipped her bird into the doll dresser which was full of clothes her mother kept on sewing, although Phyllis did not play with dolls. As she continued to open and close the drawer, the feathers twisted and bent. This she could not allow.

Phyllis pictured the scrapbook that lay on a shelf next to her mother's bed. *Baby* flowed in gilt letters across the pale blue cover.

In less than a minute Phyllis was running to her room, clamping the scrapbook to her chest. She closed her door, sat on the floor, the book on her outstretched legs. The first page gave his name: *"Arthur: Celtic -admirable, marvelous,"* then prints of two perfect baby feet, perfect baby hands. Inside were the statistics: date and time of birth, weight, then lists of food, shots, time of hair cuts, time of the dentist's visits. No mention of the relentless progress of malformation as his bones grew long while the affected muscles tightened, just empty pages for the things he could not do…. Arthur was not meant to be held in the pages of a book for ordinary babies. Phyllis felt her hands grow cold as she took out the dead pages: not Arthur, not things to keep. The wastebasket waited for them.

Phyllis pasted in her living bird.

When Arthur's book was hidden, Phyllis went to his room,

quiet except for the clicking of old Miss Bitzer's knitting nee-
dles. She was looking at the sock in her lap. A wisp of gray-
white hair had come unpinned from the bun at her neck.
"Arthur's been wanting something. I suppose it's you."

"Arthur," He jerked his head up and smiled. "I'm coming
back later. I've got something to give you."

She must wait until Miss Bitzer left his room.

●

Arthur waited. As the clock chimed six, he watched Miss
Bitzer going away, the back of her dress wrinkled from long
sitting.

Hugging the book against her body, Phyllis came to the top
of the ramp. "I've got something for you." She came close and
put the book in his lap, upside down. Trying to turn it right, his
left arm moved sideways as his right hand hit down on top.
Then, so easily, Phyllis turned it around. She stood on one foot,
then the other, but she did not lift the cover. He hit it with his
arm; clumsy. He concentrated, hitting his fist, over and over,
hitting sideways at the cover, trying to get his crooked fingers
underneath it. Phyllis only watched. *Keep trying*—she thought.

His rapid motion slowed. He worked a knuckle under the
cover, flipped it. For a moment the cover balanced vertically as
Arthur and Phyllis watched intently to see if it would fall open
or closed. They held their breath—until—"I—did. I—did—it."
Arthur's breath released, and the feathers came alive in
response. "I—found—the—bird." Phyllis heard him easily,
even without the hard sounds like *d* and *t*.

While he watched, Phyllis's face dimmed out of focus and
lacy flecks of light appeared in front of it. He felt boundaries
between them disappearing. "Aah—" But he did not have the
words to tell what was happening. Phyllis was smiling, and he
saw love in her face. "You—see—*me*," he said. But he did not
know if she understood. She sat by him for a long time as he
made his hand move slowly, gently down to the bird and

stroked the soft feathers with his knuckles. "You—gave—me—a—live—bird," he said. He looked up at Phyllis, wanting his face to say more than his words.

Phyllis stretched over his chair; she kissed his cheek. Arthur kept his fist pressed to his cheek while he watched her go, then looked back to his bird.

•

The following morning Phyllis stood outside her room. From the dark of the hall she could see her bed, still unmade, the sheet naked white in the early sun. Her mother was leaving Arthur's room. "I'll be back in a moment, dear Arthur, and I do hope you will eat a little more egg. Miss Bitzer and I do want you to stay strong and healthy."

Phyllis was haunted by the image of *BABY* on the cover of the stolen book as she watched her mother coming toward her down the hall. *No, don't!* Submerged in fear she flattened herself against the wall and watched. Her mother turned into Phyllis's room. As though guided by the focus of Phyllis's attention, Mrs. Dean leaned and reached into the waste basket. She straightened up, holding the pages of Arthur's baby book!

Her mother's steps stamped the flowers on the hall runner, pounding anger, coming toward her. The doorbell rang, but her mother ignored it. She stared straight at Phyllis who was still pressed against the wall. Phyllis stared past her mother, straining her ears for a distracting sound from the front hall. She heard the kitchen door, then Hilda's tread crossing the floor, but her mother spoke before the door was opened. "You have done a very wicked thing."

"I'm sorry," Phyllis muttered. She could see by her mother's tight face that the apology was not enough. "I won't do it again." Phyllis heard the front door close.

"Of course not, the deed..."

She was interrupted by Hilda's voice from the landing of the front steps. "Mrs. Dean, your mother-in-law is here to see you."

"I must go down stairs now, but we shall need to have a serious discussion. This act cannot go unpunished."

Mrs. Dean's footsteps faded down the stairs.

Out of the fuzz of distant sound, Phyllis recognized her Grandmother Dean's voice. Wanting to overhear, Phyllis trailed the voices through the long living room, ducking behind furniture, to the sun porch.

"Do you think Phyllis could..." But the rest of her grandmother's sentence disappeared with her around the glass door between the living room and the sun porch. Phyllis crept closer and slipped behind the portiere, scarcely disturbing the heavy brocade.

Her mother and her grandmother were standing in front of the Boston fern. Phyllis listened, watching her grandmother's lips as she spoke. Her mother's back was toward her, straight and still as furniture except for fingers that moved over the bun at the back of her neck hunting for hair pins to push tighter. "...this vale of tears..."

Phyllis saw her grandmother's eyes enlarged through heavy lenses. Her straight lips stretched away the wrinkles that puckered her mouth as if for a kiss. Her loose hair was the color of old linen. "Oh, pshaw!" Her grandmother's hand snapped down as though erasing Mrs. Dean's words. "You can be 'guided through this vale of tears' if you like. I'd rather 'have a circus'." Light glinted from her glasses as she tossed her head.

Mrs. Dean retreated into an awkward silence, then, lacking words of her own, recited familiar ones. "I admire your valiant spirit in the face of life's slings and arrows, but under these circumstances, I find revelry a difficult retreat. 'Bread and circuses'..."

"In my time of life, revelry is an advance. Not a retreat. And I think Phyllis could use some happy sparks in her life too. I'd like to borrow her company for a day or two."

Phyllis felt her mother's *no* close under her "Perhaps, considering your unfortunate circumstances, we could work it out. But..."

"You know I do not wish to be coddled. It would be a good idea in any circumstances."

"But not until evening. Phyllis and I must first attend to a little problem." *Big* swelled up to hide her mother's *little*. "Her father will bring her to you when he comes home from work."

With dread, she heard the closing of the front door, then, "Phyllis." Her mother's call came from the library, that perfect room of muted colors in satin paint and sets of classics bound in leather and gold perfectly straight on the shelves. She would have to... Slowly she unwound herself from the portiere and shuffled across the living room, through the front hall, into the library.

Mrs. Dean pointed to the needlepoint-covered seat of the youth chair, and Phyllis obediently sat. "I'm sure you know what I wish to talk to you about?"

She looked past her mother to stare at the immaculate Venus, her severed arms, neatly cut away; *can't steal with cutoff arms.*

"Do you have anything to tell me?"

Nothing. Phyllis continued to stare at the cut off arms.

"This very unfortunate act has made it clear that I have somehow failed to teach you the importance of honesty—and the sacredness of private property." She hesitated, finished brokenly, "Why? What made you destroy—*this*?" She held out the torn pages.

Phyllis murmured into her lap. "They just came out. I'm sorry."

"The little foot print, that perfect little foot; it is torn. What made you do such a thing?"

Phyllis remained a silent statue of herself, staring in confused disbelief at the torn page.

"Phyllis, please answer me."

"I didn't know."

"You did not know what? That this was not yours to destroy?"

Phyllis shook her head.

"Phyllis, Phyllis, you are such an enigma! What am I to do with you?"

Phyllis hung her head so that her hair hid her face.

"What have you done with the book?"

Phyllis gave her mother a fearfully silent look.

"Since you have nothing to say to me, I see no object in continuing this conversation. Please go to your room. You can expect to stay there for the rest of the day. Hilda will bring you your lunch. I hope that by evening you will have gained in understanding and be ready to explain your actions to your father and me."

The long morning, the long afternoon, waiting for her father…

Phyllis had no hope that he would do other than support her mother. Early in Phyllis's life her father had given up the fight to free his daughter from her mother's control. The first big argument had been about kindergarten. "But she is such a baby!" her mother had exclaimed. Her father and her grandmother feared that she would have trouble adjusting to school if she started behind her contemporaries. As they predicted, Phyllis felt small and out of place in Crest School for girls. Believing that she was keeping her daughter safe, Mrs. Dean had endeavored to delay Phyllis's maturation and restrain her from escaping the smothering wings of motherhood. As a result, she entered first grade without knowing how to read or write a single word, an outsider in the community of Crest girls who were expected to excel in academic achievement. In the corridors she walked close to the walls, pressing herself away from the stream of chattering classmates. Even in her careful printing she tried to make herself invisible, and in third grade Miss Brown told her to write larger as her glasses were not strong enough to magnify Phyllis's letters to legibility.

But her grandmother, and nearly as important, Fang, the stuffed polar bear cub looking out of Grandmother's bricked up fireplace, had always been a safe part of Phyllis's world. She thought of the front door opening and Fang to welcome her. That vision helped her endure the long slow afternoon.

Her father slammed the door *before* the clock chimed five.

Her mother would still be in the kitchen talking to Hilda. Phyllis was packed and ready. She grabbed her suitcase and stumbled down the stairs holding onto the banister to keep from falling when the suitcase bumped her legs. She dropped it at the bottom of the stairs and dashed to meet him, "I'm going to Grandma's," she said breathlessly.

"Yes, I know. Grandma called me."

Phyllis clutched his hand, hoping to rush away before her mother could tell him what she had done.

"Wait a bit," her father said, "I'm going to say goodbye to Arthur."

●

He saw his father standing, so big, on the ramp above him. Then Father said their joke. "Hello there old man."

"—Aahh."

"You mean to tell me I'm the old man and you're the smart young fellow?"

"—Aahh."

"Well then, I'd say a smart young fellow needs some fresh air. Outside it's a beautiful warm evening. I'll open this window." He was tugging up the tight sash on the garden side. "There's a nice little breeze to let in for you to enjoy."

His father kept on talking, but Arthur heard the wind rustle his oak's leaves, bringing its words to his skin. They told him *come*. Bugs were saying it too, in squeaky voices.

Without sound Arthur made his mind tell them *can't*.

In a long-ago voice his father said, "The night felt like this when Tom and I set off for the Arctic. A night full of promise." When he said *promise,* his voice dropped into a sad hole. Arthur didn't hear his father after that. *Come out* was shouting at him too loud.

Phyllis was standing on one foot, then the other at the top of the ramp. "It's time to take me to Grandma's," she interrupted.

"I—go—too." Nobody listened.

"Good bye, young fellow. We'll talk arctic adventure on another day. Now don't let the polar bears get you."

"I'm—like—you," Arthur said to the wind. "Nobody—listens—nobody—knows." Like fur and feathers the wind was soft. "But—I've—got—a—storm."

Arthur let it crack out through him in a moaning call. No one heard.

●

Phyllis and her father had reached the bottom of the steps. Phyllis picked up her suitcase and tried to run with it to the door. "Wait a minute, young lady. We haven't said *goodbye* to your mother."

"Do we have to?" She didn't speak loud enough to penetrate his impaired hearing. He was already opening the door into the back hall.

Her mother heard him right away. She came from the kitchen, her arms clamped stiffly to her sides. "I have something important you should know." The three of them stood in the front hall. Phyllis felt her mother's eyes, like Hilda's ice pick, all the way into the bad thing she had done.

"It's Phyllis?" her father questioned.

Her mother said the whole thing right away. Phyllis tried not to hear it again.

"Yes, this is important, but I will have to discuss this with Phyllis in the car. Unfortunately I have an appointment with a tent-show man who needs advice about waterproofing his big top, so I will be rushed to make it back to dinner."

"Oh dear, what an unfortunate time for you to be rushed." She rubbed her hands together as though she were washing them.

"It can't be helped." He looked down at Phyllis. "Now, Miss…" The thin line of his lips made her chest shake, and she ducked her head and squeezed her mouth in fear.

But even though he knew it all, his manners did not change.

"May I carry your suitcase?" He took it, and she shuffled behind, her face hidden by her bush of curls.

He did not say any more until they were in the car. He drove slowly, glancing down at her. "Why did you tear up Arthur's book, Phyllis?"

For my bird, for Arthur, for a way to keep it safe.

"Please tell me, Phyllis."

"I didn't tear it."

"You took the pages out." He paused. Slowly Phyllis nodded her head. "And the page with the footprints was torn."

After a long painful pause, she answered, "Maybe the wastebasket tore it. I hurried. I don't know."

Phyllis looked at the trees; a green tent passing over them. Not much farther. Almost there.

"Were you angry at Arthur, is that why you tore it?"

Phyllis squeezed the tears back. "No. It's different." It felt as though her breath was bumping her words. "I can't tell why." She thought about the book in Arthur's room where she had hidden it under papers. *What would he think if she told him?... maybe... Could she...?*

But his voice exploded. "You don't know!" Frustration spilled through his control, wiping out Phyllis's budding courage.

The car pulled to the curb. Phyllis could see bits of dark green siding behind the crooked trees. Her father gripped her suitcase. "I can take it," she offered tentatively.

"I wouldn't think of it! No lady carries her own luggage when she travels with me."

As she stood on the walk to her grandmother's house, she gathered strength from anticipation of freedom from her parents' grip. "Please no. I want to carry it. I want to go by myself."

The long walkway, up the steps, across the porch, the suitcase bumping her legs, her father close behind, watching. As the door swung back, Olga's wide, white uniform filled the opening as it did on her father's birthday and at Christmas. "Well, well, well. Phyllis! Come right in, your grandma's looking for you." Phyllis ducked away from Olga's hug, not wanting her face to be smothered between Olga's pillow breasts.

"Mr. Dean, it's always so good to have you come."

"How is she?" he asked, concerned.

Phyllis was accustomed to adults talking over her head, and she had learned not to pay attention. She greeted Fang, "Hi." The cub stood directly opposite the front door, denned in a glass case with the red bricks of the fireplace behind it.

"Your grandma's laying on the couch listening to one of them symphonies and just waiting for you to come," Olga said.

Grandmother Dean's head was propped against a pile of darkly faded pillows, her eyes closed, her mouth slightly open, the corners wet, like Arthur's. "Grandmother..." she asked softly.

"Ah, who's that?" Phyllis watched her grandmother's eyes pop open and her mouth close. She rubbed the red places on her nose where her glasses usually rested, then sat up. "Well, Phyllis, you're just the person I'm most glad to see." Asking quickly while she put on her glasses, "Is your father with you?"

"I'm right here." He snapped to attention. "Delivered, one granddaughter to Mrs. Dean." He shed his martial sobriety, and his mouth skewed into a half smile. He leaned over and kissed his mother.

"Will you sit down for a while? Stay for dinner?"

Please say "no." Just go and don't tell her about me.

"Not this time. I'll save it for a night when you aren't so well entertained."

Phyllis followed her grandmother upstairs to her father's old room. The mirror over the dresser reflected a window behind Phyllis's head, and the branches of a fir tree seemed to extend the bush of her hair. Out of a frame in the center of the dresser, a boy's face smiled down from a pattern of leaves. Phyllis pointed. "Is that his tree?"

Grandmother returned the boy's smile. "His tree house. To build it he used one of the leaves from the dining-room table, but it was in the basement, and he didn't know," she said. "I didn't have the heart to scold him. Here..." Her grandmother pointed through the window to the oak in front of the garage. "You can still see his tree. It was the envy of the neighborhood." Her voice dropped into the past. "I remember it strung with vines of boys. So many they could pull each other up to the house without using the steps. I trusted their survival."

"Now it's mostly dead. Why?"

"A long time ago it was struck by lightning."

After dinner Phyllis watched a ceremony: Olga brought a glass of water with little bubbles sparkling on the sides, then stood a little way back as the hand with bones and veins showing through the skin picked up a white capsule, then a red one. Like taking communion, she took them both at once, and then she sipped the water.

In the fading light, they went to look at John Dean's tree. There was a round scar half way up the trunk with a roll of bark, like thick lips, surrounding it. The branches were stubby where they had been trimmed, and some high up were dead.

"It keeps on, year after year, injured and scarred but never dying."

Phyllis stroked the old bark. She felt its age, already a big tree when her father was little.

"Here's one of the steps your father nailed into the trunk." The gray wood was split next to the nail heads. "But it's not strong enough to climb any more."

Phyllis leaned over and gazed into the hollow center. "The cave looks big enough to sit in, but it's burned dirty," Phyllis said. "It needs a window."

"You can make one tomorrow."

●

In the morning Phyllis woke expecting to start right in on her tree project, but her grandmother had forgotten. Instead, she announced that she was going to the doctor's. "Olga reminded me of it this morning."

Phyllis clamped her mouth shut, then crossed the hall and lay on her stomach in front of the bear cub's glass case. She looked into the cub's eyes, like yellow jelly. After a long time she could see them move, and the cub lived for her. Fang, like Santa's reindeer, was a perennial fixture of the North, a story that could never change: *The day Fang's mother was killed, whiteness was all there was over the clean world. Father in white fur clothes hunting a bear that was all white. White tracks over white snow, up white hills and into white valleys. Then a face marked black on white like the coal face of a snowman.*

"I've never told you the whole story of Fang." Phyllis felt her grandmother's eyes behind her, watching the back of her head. "But now I want you to hear it all, and remember. I want you to be able to tell Arthur. He's a boy like his father. He should know, and now that you're nine-years old, you're big enough to tell him."

"Arthur has a friend-tree out his window. He told me. But he couldn't have a tree house like father." Phyllis rolled over and looked up at her grandmother. "I remember how Father took care of the little bear and fed him with a bottle…. Just like I could see it. Like the picture in Arthur's bear scrapbook."

"No," Grandmother said. "It wasn't like that. He didn't have a bottle. I think you remember a fairy story. Let me tell you all of it just the way it was."

Phyllis shook her head; her hair flipped *no* against her cheeks.

"I can see so clearly the day your father left for the Canadian Arctic. He was a grown man, but still he looked just like that picture on his dresser, a smile with a space between his two front teeth. So much hope and so full of pride…as if he had just built the best tree house a boy ever saw. I shared his joy, glad that he was going." Phyllis didn't like the sound of her grandmother's funny little laugh when she said *glad*. "It was your father's first real job after he was released from the navy—1919 I believe it was—something to do with communication. Funny, I can't remember whether it was with the telephone company or something wireless. He went with Tom. Perhaps your father has told you about Tom?"

Phyllis shook her head.

"He was your father's roommate all through college and his best friend. I don't think he's ever had a really good friend since, but Tom..." Grandmother stopped talking, and the silence was like the times with Arthur when she could feel the sadness inside him.

"The first letter I got from your father was full of enthusiasm for his new life. It was mailed from Baffin Island. That's way north, across from Greenland. He actually wrote it in an Eskimo's igloo, and it smelled fishy. I suppose it was too cold in that ice house for him to wash his hands. Your father told me he had hitched a ride to the igloo with a man heading north, I suppose on a dog sled. He took rice and sugar and dried fruit to trade for the loan of a sled and dog team for hunting. He lived in the igloo for a week or more learning how to drive the dogs." Her voice dropped low. "The last sentence of that letter: 'After a rib-sticking meal that chewed like rubber and tasted like whale hide, Tom and I are heading out on a polar-bear hunt.' I didn't get another letter."

Phyllis heard and felt the dead quiet of snow. She shivered. *I want the old story. Without Tom.* "Did he go too?" she asked. In the reflection on Fang's glass case she saw her grandmother nod.

"It was a month after I got the letter. Your father came home. So changed. He..."

Her voice became strong again. "He didn't tell it all at once. The story came out in bits and pieces over many days.

"The day of the hunt was bad; they never should have started. A fog over everything, an icy kind of fog that caught the light and scattered it so that there was only brilliance without form. Polar bears have no enemies; there is no fear in them. They may attack anything that moves, and they can run much faster than a man." In the space of her Grandmother's pause, Phyllis must hear, feel and wait for the answer she already dreaded.

"With Baffin Bay on one side of them and a rocky wall on the other, Tom and your father were picking a path between chunks of ice. Not quiet the way you'd expect; it was noisy all the time with the rumbling and grinding of ice. Ice blocks everywhere, and finally one of them jammed the runners of the sled so that the dogs couldn't pull it. Your father stayed behind with the dogs, to try and free the sled…" In the pause before she continued, Phyllis saw her grandmother's eyes get wet and shinier than Fang's yellow ones. "But Tom walked ahead to look for a passable way. Your father watched him climbing over an ice block, holding his rifle high so as not to knock it against the ice.

"He didn't see it happen…"

Then Grandmother started over in another place. "Your father had a beard when he came home. I could imagine it white and sharp with icicles. He was standing in the hall. I asked for Tom. Your father said very little, but I remember it all: 'Tom is dead. A bear. I heard him call. I heard him, but the sled was almost free. I took just a few seconds, not even a minute. It was too long. When I climbed over the ice chunks in front of me, I saw him. The bear was on him. I shot, but it was too late. Tom was dead.'

"Your father never knew how it happened. Tom called your father's name just once, never fired a shot.

"Your father worked the sled over to Tom. Tom dead, the bear dead. A cub was trying to nurse from its dead mother. Too little even to growl. Your father couldn't leave it. He tied it on the sled. It took a long time because the dogs went wild over it. Back at the igloo, he tried to feed it canned milk with a spoon. Without a bottle, he must have spilled most of it.

"The cub died in less than a week.

"He took the cub to a taxidermist in Goose Bay and had it stuffed. I don't think it was a good idea. To keep it with him like that. Reminding him of Tom. But there was nothing I could do. He was set. John got that way—Set. And there was nothing anyone could do."

Grandmother's voice became crisp and close. "It was soon afterwards that he married your mother. Beautiful as a statue," she added. "A year later Arthur was born."

Olga was waiting behind Grandmother Dean. "David has the car out front. You'll be late."

"Oh pshaw!" She walked quickly and picked up her big black purse from the bench in the hall.

Through the living room window, Phyllis watched the car drive away with her grandmother. *I liked it when I was young.* She felt a foreboding that expanded beyond the loss of the old story.

Without her grandmother, she went into the backyard and stopped under her father's tree. She looked up at the weathered boards of the old tree house, then into the black hollow, feeling the pressure of a serious job awaiting her.

After examining several stones by the garage, Phyllis discovered a sharp one, then spent a very long time scraping at the charred wood.

Too hard! Angrily she threw the stone against the tree.

When, finally, she heard the car return, Phyllis ran to her grandmother gesticulating her plan with sooty hands and explaining in scattered words.

"Wait a minute." Grandmother stood still. "What's this you want?"

"The tree's still black and dirty; I can't get it clean."

"Maybe we can't get it really clean. But for now let's go have our lunch, and afterwards we'll see."

"Will David still be here? He could saw a window."

Grandmother shook her head. "David is busy washing the car. You don't need him. You'll make your own window."

"But I don't know how."

"You can learn."

●

The hatchet was beside her, two blisters on her hand. A finger of light reached into the tree, and Phyllis could look through the jagged hole with one eye. Grandmother sat on the grass. Phyllis saw *tired,* tired all over: closed eyes tired of seeing, and muscles hanging down tired of the bones.

Phyllis left the tree, sat down beside her grandmother who seemed to listen to her even before she spoke. Phyllis stammered out a question she did not know how to ask.

"It's hard," Grandmother Dean responded. "Ideas go in and out of words like air through open windows."

They spent time saying nothing at all, Phyllis's grandmother trying to imagine the unasked questions.

"People don't speak the things in the center of them. But sometimes, if you're lucky, you can feel them and, through another, know a bigger part of yourself."

"But they don't tell me. Grown-ups hide important things. Like I'm too little to know, even when I'm nine."

"They don't want to tell you I'm going to die. That's all. I feel fine now, but I have a disease called cancer."

Phyllis shook her head, not ready to accept the casual remark.

Her grandmother continued. "We all die sometime, and it's a splendid thing. It keeps us from getting older and older until there's no fun left in living."

Phyllis felt a creeping emptiness.

"But I won't die for a long time. For you, a long time." She stood up and walked toward the house.

●

David drove Phyllis home. Her grandmother stayed in the car and waved at Mrs. Dean when she opened the heavy door then closed it behind Phyllis.

"Did you have a good time?"

"Yes." The rest she would tell to Arthur.

Phyllis opened her suitcase but put nothing away. She looked out of her window at the top branches of Arthur's white oak

and beyond to a small piece of sky framed by crooked branches. Looking at the sky through that little frame was like looking at her grandmother through the little window of the tree
cave, seeing only a small part of something big. Phyllis stirred
the mix of images in her mind. Did people have frames around
them—like windows with the shades down. What was inside
the frames of people, waiting to be seen? Phyllis thought of
Arthur needing a window in the wall of himself.

●

Arthur was lying in his bed in his night room waiting for
Miss Bitzer and his mother to put him in his chair and wheel
him across the hall and down the ramp into his day room.

I am a strong man. Arthur's dream was a real piece of his life
even after he woke up. *I want people to know.* But Phyllis would
not be home from Grandmother's until almost night, and the
powerful image was bursting to be told. In his dream he was a
tall big man, as big as Carl, with a pointed nose and a mus-
tache. Water was all around him, and he was standing up in the
bow of a big gray battleship with guns poking out from every
side. He was standing high on the bow, but the stern of the
ship was sinking into the wavy blue ocean. All day he thought
about it. He felt only strong; he was not afraid.

When evening came he sat by the window waiting for Phyllis.
He saw his sister come up the walk with her suitcase, but she
was fuzzy from the mist he had breathed on the glass. He
licked it clear with his tongue, and then he knew how he would
show her his picture.

She came into his room. She tried to talk, but Arthur waved
his arms and his legs at her. Then she listened.

"I—dream—a—picture." His mouth would not form any
sharp sounds, so he had to say it over and over before Phyllis
could understand.

"I—want—to—paint."

Phyllis shook her head until Arthur opened his mouth and

closed it like a bite. Then she knew, and she brought her box of paints, paper, a glass of water and a brush.

"This handle is too pointed, but I can break it." Arthur watched the handle snap. As Phyllis dipped the brush in the water, his apprehension mounted. "What color would you like?"

"Gray."

He saw the soft bristles slide over the little square of black water color. He clamped his teeth on the handle so hard that he feared he would bite it in two.

Slowly: the top of the deck in a jerky line, tight like jagged lightening. But, before the line had reached to where the ocean would be, a stream of saliva ran down the handle of the brush, and the color washed to a muddy pool.

Arthur let the brush drop from his teeth. There were tears in his eyes. His ship had to stay in his head.

"Maybe you can try again."

Arthur said *no* with a wilted shudder. Phyllis did not urge him. It was getting late, and she had a message for him. "But now I've got something to tell you," she said.

He looked at her. Nothing good. "No."

"But Grandma said. It's about Fang and Father. She wants me to tell you the whole different story."

Arthur's objections bristled out of him; he did not care where his mad came from, the painting or the story.

"Tom was there too."

I know Tom. Dad told me. His pal. He saw Phyllis shake her head. *Now more bad.* Arthur wanted Phyllis to get the baby bear sucking on a bottle in his bear scrapbook. He tried to ask her, but she wouldn't wait. She told him the bad dying instead.

Arthur saw the changed story in his head—just how it looked. He knew from pictures in a magazine that had been on his tray underneath his glass of orange juice. It had pictures of war. Arthur remembered the blood. Now he saw the bear claws open Tom's blood, bullets open the bear's blood. The red of it splashed on his father, splashed through Arthur's mind so that when he closed his eyes, red was a big puddle—like his painting. Then he saw the little cub. It was trying to nurse from its dead mother.

"Eeh—"sucking dead blood. At the image, a spastic contraction shook his body.

Before Arthur had time to talk, their mother called; so Phyllis had to go to her room. Mrs. Dean was standing beside Phyllis's suitcase. "What have you been doing? All this time wasted, and you have not unpacked a thing. Now it is your bedtime."

●

Breakfast was almost always silent.

Mr. Dean's face was screened behind his paper. After a long time he put it down and asked, "Well now, what did you and your grandmother do all day?"

"I made a window in your tree. Then we talked."

Her father was waiting for more.

"Grandmother says she's going to die."

"Whatever could..." Mrs. Dean exploded, then looked at Phyllis and clamped her mouth shut.

"Now Deirdre, we haven't heard all Phyllis has to say."

Mrs. Dean was crumpling and uncrumpling her napkin. "But a child should not be told such things!"

"And I suppose we are going to save her from mortality," her father muttered.

Phyllis heard only the *we*. "I know that Grandmother has cancer. But you don't have to worry. She won't die for a long time," Phyllis said calmly, proud of her new knowledge.

The word *cancer* hung in the air, and Phyllis felt it. She frowned and ran her fingers up through her curls. "Grandmother thought it would be all right," she said, "like it was supposed to be—not for a long time. But dying would be a good idea when she wasn't having fun any more."

Mr. Dean's spoon scraped up the last bite of Red River cereal. Staring into his empty bowl he said softly, "That's my plucky mother."

Phyllis felt his sadness. "We'll miss her, won't we?"

"We certainly will," her father said. He walked around the table, leaned over and kissed Phyllis's forehead.

When she looked up at him, Phyllis's eyes filled with tears. "Then your birthday and Christmas will be all different, won't it?"

He nodded. He opened his mouth, but he didn't say anything. Phyllis filled the silence.

"We talked about Tom too, and I told Arthur. He's supposed to know because he's a boy like you. Grandmother said."

"What business does she have... This could only upset and confuse his poor mind. As if my dear boy doesn't have troubles enough!"

Her husband talked on top of her words. "Who knows how much Arthur understands? At least Mother treats him as an important person who needs to be informed."

Before Mrs. Dean could respond, he abruptly switched subjects. "I have something special for Arthur," he said, "but first, I have some special news for both of you. *You too, Deirdre.*" There were barbs in his emphasis. Phyllis listened closely. "You'll never guess who I found to take care of your grandmother." He smiled at Phyllis.

"Tell me. I can't guess."

"Someone you knew a long time ago." Phyllis shook her head. "Someone with a bird."

It took a little while for Phyllis's memory to catch up to her father's wide smile, then came the excitement he was expecting. "Edie! Can I go see her?"

Phyllis's enthusiasm drowned out her mother's "John! What can you be thinking of? I know you disapproved of my letting her go, but..."

He ignored her and focused on Phyllis. "The next time we go to Grandma's. Now for Arthur's surprise, something in the back of my closet that I've been saving for Christmas. But now is the right time."

Phyllis followed her father past her mother's room to his

room where the walls were gray-blue and the bedspread and curtains were dark maroon. It smelled of shaving cream. He disappeared behind his closet door, then came out with a large box. Phyllis and her mother followed him into Arthur's room.

"This was going to be your Christmas present," he said, "but I didn't think you'd mind getting it early, especially if I forget, come Christmas, that I've already given you something."

Expectancy jerked Arthur's body as he watched his father take out his pocket-knife and cut the twine. His excited squeal greeted the revelation: "Aah—ou—aa—oo!"

"Every young fellow needs a radio," he said as he plugged it in.

A hearty male voice commanded, "Stretch up and touch your toes; stretch up and touch your toes...."

"That one we don't need." Mr. Dean turned the dial to a music station, and when they left, Arthur was listening to a polka on his own radio.

●

It was only two weeks after her visit with her grandmother. Phyllis was sitting in Miss Bitzer's chair.

"There—is—something—funny."

"Something funny? I don't get it."

"For—a—long—time. People—different."

Phyllis nodded. "Since the last time I stayed at Grandma's house... Since then everything turned different. Sometimes I get scared. I don't want her to die. But she told me it was going to be a long time. Now I wonder. Sometimes I get this feeling I won't get to see Edie."

"I—don't—like—that."

"But she told me. She said she won't die for a longtime. She promised."

Phyllis was working to hold back her tears when their mother came into the room. "Phyllis, dear child, could you please come with me for a few minutes?"

Phyllis followed her mother into her room. She sat in the

rose-bud chair beside the chaise lounge. Her mother sat, very strait, on the edge of the chaise. "I have some very sad news."

Phyllis didn't tell her mother she already knew what it was. "Where's father?"

"He is busy making arrangements. This afternoon your father and I are going to say *good bye* to Grandmother."

"You mean she's just going away?" Phyllis asked hopefully.

"In a way, she has already gone. She passed away last night in her sleep." She added hastily, "I am sure she felt no pain."

"You mean she died?"

Her mother stood up and went to Phyllis, ready to comfort her. But Phyllis darted away to Arthur's room, her mother following. "Phyllis," her mother called, "Arthur does not need to go through this pain."

Phyllis had reached the top of the ramp. "We already knew," she said.

Slowly she followed Phyllis to Arthur. Rooted between her two children, after a long silence, she said, "It is difficult to know the right thing to say. She gave Arthur an agitated kiss, then Phyllis. "'The Lord giveth, and the Lord taketh away. Blessed be the name of the Lord'."

Phyllis wanted to be alone with Arthur. She knew she was about to cry, but she didn't want to be weak in front of her mother. "It's okay for you to go now," she said in a choked voice.

Reluctantly their mother left the room murmuring softly, "Dear boy, Dear boy, I so wished to spare you the pain."

Phyllis sat by Arthur, and they both wept quietly for a long time.

September, 1934

Two months after her grandmother died, Phyllis stood, small, in the doorway watching her mother pack. The usual order of her mother's room was hidden under suitcases, clothes and tissue paper. "It is so difficult to go away. All the planning… Now do practice your dancing lessons, dear. They will help improve your posture." Mrs. Dean pulled nervously at the short fingers of her left hand. "I am so fortunate to have a kind generous father to go home to. I am forever grateful to him for giving me so much, even his own home, this beautiful house."

Kind? Phyllis saw her grandfather as a black vest stuffed with a long slow voice, lugubrious, like a minister she couldn't understand.

"When do you go away?"

"Four thirty five. But I do need help." She waved a hand that moved loosely, like tissue paper. "Could you please ask Hilda to come and help me finish?"

●

Mrs. Dean was in Boston for a week, leaving a strange difference in the air of the house, like a classroom with the teacher gone, yet with some order clinging, a party mood, yet quiet, still afraid of noise.

Phyllis stood in the archway between the hall and the living room. She looked down at her black tights and pink leotard, then moved self-consciously across the floor. Unaccustomed dimness in the room sharpened her vision. The lamp shade by her mother's place on the couch was dark. The soft slap of new cards was familiar, and she watched her father's golden-clean hands in the circle of light from his desk lamp. The left hand was quiet, the right tapped the desk—finger after finger after finger, again, again, and again. For a long time she watched the movement that was and had been since she could first remember.

Then quickly, suddenly, the cards were swept up and tapped into a sharp rectangle. They were not set out again. The right arm reached up so that the coat sleeve shortened, showing the cold shine of a cuff-link. Then Phyllis noticed the glass, amber and dewed with the coolness of ice. He sipped slowly, a break from customary routine. Phyllis's eyes forgot the rest of her body until the slipping of the record she held under her arm reminded her of purpose.

She stepped closer to her father so that she would not have to speak so loudly into the church-like quiet. "Can I play a record?"

"'May' you play a record."

Phyllis stamped at this reflection of her mother, but she repeated, "May I?"

"You sure can." His smile was skewed, but soft in the dim light. "Are you going to dance for me?"

"I feel funny with you watching. I'm no good yet. I need to practice."

"I'd like to watch you anyway." Her father pushed his chair back. Phyllis ran to the phonograph, her body tense with contained action. "This is the best, "Les Sylphides." I mean it's the best one we have for dancing. I haven't found any others. Sibelius…" She wrinkled her nose.

Her father refilled his glass from a pinched bottle at the back of his desk, then moved to the fireplace, taking the glass and the bottle with him. A fire was laid, logs white and clean behind the polished andirons. Phyllis watched her father take a match from the mantle and light the crumpled paper. "Your mother will doubtless complain of smoke on the andirons, but if we don't burn this soon, Hilda will have to dust the birch."

He laughed, and Phyllis laughed with him. She turned on the new record player and watched the arm swing into place. With the first notes, she forgot her father and listened with her body, yet only in fleeting seconds did she escape from her self-consciousness enough to melt into the music.

When the record ended, her father's clapping hands offered more approval than she was ready to accept. The wall she set up to resist censure was so thick that approval, also, was walled out.

"You did a good job."

She hung her head modestly. "No, I didn't." *But I'm going to learn.* The thought felt good, and very quietly she said it out loud.

"Of course you are."

She looked up quickly, and a smile flashed across her face.

Flushed from her dancing, she lay on her back, listening to the almost-quiet and watching the fire. The light shone bright and orange on her father's glass. Between sips, he was talking softly to the glass, as though Phyllis were not in the room.

"Even filled with ice you're warmer company than she…" He raised his head but looked past Phyllis to the black glass of the window. "Phyllis, do you know your mother?"

The question did not need an answer. He was not looking at Phyllis. He looked into his glass, and his voice came from a long time ago. "She was my new wife. She was beautiful, and I wanted her. And she stood there white and still, like a gardenia. A gardenia that turns brown when you touch it. A gardenia." His voice was so quiet Phyllis could scarcely hear it. But then it became loud. "A goddamned untouchable gardenia. Just a goddamned fancied-up mushroom!"

He turned his head and looked into his daughter's wide-open eyes.

He put his glass down, got up, stood still for just a moment, then left the room with careful steps. He had not told her to go to bed, but she knew it was past time.

The hall was dark. She reminded herself she was too old for dragons.

III

June, 1939

For a quick moment before it disappeared behind the spring-green leaves of his oak tree, Arthur saw an airplane shining against the sky. Through his open window he heard it, loud and steady, then dying away. He was alone; there was no one to tell. He wanted to paint a picture of it, but he needed Phyllis to help.

The old pictures of sheep and children singing in church that Miss Bitzer put on his bulletin board were gone now. Arthur looked at his own pictures. The very first one he ever painted, after Phyllis fixed his brushes, was a long-ago dream. He was standing on the bow of his ship, up there big and strong. It looked like he had one leg and his head was square, but he was straight and tall. The ocean was clear blue. The lines of the ship wiggled, but there were no puddles, and the thick guns sticking out made it easy to tell that it was a battleship. When he looked at it, Arthur remembered how good he felt back then when he was a little kid twelve years old. He liked to see how much better his ships had become.

He would paint the blue sky first and after it was really dry, he would paint the airplane with his silver paint, and leaves would be all around it. He tried to call Phyllis with his mind. She did not come to help him as much as she used to right after she thought of wrapping the handles of his brushes so that the paint did not wash into puddles. He looked at everything on the table against the wall underneath his pictures, too far away to reach: paper, paints, strips of terrycloth, safety pins, brushes and his book, *Anyone Can Draw*. Phyllis gave it to him for his seventeenth birthday way last January. Now some of the pages were torn and folded because he turned them himself.

Near the end of the book, he found people without any clothes on. The woman was his favorite, and he painted a picture of her with pink paint. Miss Bitzer helped him, but she didn't pay attention, and she only saw the picture upside down. Phyllis was surprised when he showed her, and she told him not to show Mother. Then she said he better paint something else, and she kept the picture.

A long time went by, and he got tired of looking at his old pictures. His cuckoo came out of his hole three times, and it was after ten o'clock in the morning. Then Phyllis came.

"I—want—to—paint."

"I don't know…" She stopped listening. She was looking out of the window with her back to him. She didn't pay attention at all.

●

Phyllis looked down into the sun-painted garden. From above, she saw seventeen-year-old George magnified by her fourteen-year-old admiration to the solidity of a Rivera mural, his back muscles swelling to the job of hoeing winter leaves into heavy clay around the base of a young mountain ash.

"I—don't—like—George." Arthur repeated, repeated many times to Phyllis's back. As she turned to face him, Arthur opened his mouth in a smile; but he saw her distant look, and his head moved rapidly from side to side.

"I woke up in the most magic sort of dream." Her misted eyes focused beyond her brother. "Everything was rosy like a sunset, and I was floating in some forever-land. Like myself, my whole self, was air, without anything heavy, no body at all, and this feeling…" Sacred, beyond clumsy words. Even *love* did not say enough.

"I—don't—like—George."

This time Phyllis's gaze shocked to attention as she grasped Arthur's meaning. Feeling his words as an attack reaching to the heart of her affections, she opened her mouth to answer; but then shut it with a snap, biting back her anger. As she hurried away up the ramp, her angry flash dissipated and disappointment took its place.

Arthur's muscles constricted, and the usual pain in his chest sharpened. *You don't know. You shouldn't like George.* His wordless voice followed Phyllis down the hall as she ran to the back door and out into the garden.

Before George saw her, Phyllis stopped to watch him work. The beat of his hoe on the earth felt like an extension of her heartbeat, the terrestrial anchor of her airy dream.

His impassive face could not hide the smile that crinkled around the glint of his blue eyes. Even when a boy—like Arthur, three years older than Phyllis—he was big enough so that a tuft of his blond hair tented up above the back of the seat as he sat beside his father in the car. The sparks from his blue eyes promised her an excitement limitless as the sky. Her old memories glowed in the light of magnified recall: George playing in the garden, under rainbows in the sprinkler, gleaming ribbons of mud shimmering between his bare toes. As though the icy sparks of the sprinkler were striking her skin, the memory sent a shiver through Phyllis that quivered her body to the tips of her fingers and toes.

In summer when school was out even her mother could not monitor Phyllis's every move. Playing in the garage with George was her favorite forbidden excitement. Her grandfather had built no ordinary garage to accommodate his collection of cars, two of the first Fords and later his treasured Pierce Arrow. Now, through Carl's and George's attention, a Cadillac and Mr. Dean's second-hand two-tone Cord roadster were kept gleaming. The garage, built on top of a hill that dropped away in a series of steep garden terraces, was designed in the shape of a three-leaf clover around a central turntable like a small version of those for turning locomotives. When George and Carl washed the cars, water poured down around the edges of the great welded turntable and splashed up an echo from mysterious depths. Mrs. Dean's dire warning added thrills of danger to the experience: "If you fell, you could horribly mutilate your hands in the gap between the floor and the turntable."

Nevertheless, whenever Carl was not there to stop them, George and Phyllis would play on "our merry-go-round." With one foot pushing on the garage floor, they spun the oiled turntable as fast as they could swing their feet. When the speed was too much for Phyllis's short legs, she would stand on the edge of the whirling disk letting George spin her faster and faster until she staggered from dizziness coupled with the excitement of danger.

Now George's back was to her. Excitement pressed upward like fizz from a shaken pop bottle. "Hi." Her voice sounded funny, mixed with bubbles.

He wheeled, then threw his hoe backwards toward the tree trunk. "Hi." He stood planted and swung his arms forward and back in unison. His face was strong and square.

She took a step toward him; he took a step toward her. They looked at each other. Too long. She giggled.

When they could not stand still any longer, George jumped to her, his hands reaching to tickle her ribs. They dropped to the ground and tussled like puppies in the newly mowed grass.

Above the upper garden terrace and behind the garage, the house loomed above them.

●

Up in Arthur's room, Miss Bitzer bent over Arthur. His new wheel chair, with a deep basket seat to hold him sitting, was lower than his old one so that his feet rested on the floor. "What are you trying to say?"

"Wino." Arthur's arms waved in too broad an arc to point, but he showed her with his eyes.

"Oh, you're trying to say window." Miss Bitzer wheeled him

to the garden side of the room, but his head was too low, and he could see only the tops of the trees.

"Closer." She pushed him close enough so that he could rest his chin on the sill.

He saw them, like fighting dogs, rolling on the ground. George held her wrists, and his face was close to her cheek. Arthur burned with a flare of anger. *maybe biting*. After while George let go and stood up.

"I—mad." There was no one to hear. Miss Bitzer had gone away and left him at the window. His blue bird came out of the clock, so Arthur talked to him without words. *Men that are big and tough and not nice, they make me mad.* Cuckoo went back into his hole before Arthur finished. His voice rose loud; like howling.

●

Down in the garden distance muted the sound from Arthur's room; birds singing their claims to nesting sites played over his wailing voice.

George's face was close, his breath was on her cheek, and the strong clean smell of him was in her nostrils mixed with Carl's pipe smoke clinging to his clothes. The strange tingling in Phyllis's body elicited a nervous laugh. As he held her hands to the ground at the side of her head, she felt her shirt stretch against her still-new breasts.

When he moved away, a cool breeze replaced the damp heat of his body. As they stood awkwardly apart, Phyllis hung her head, then saw that one shirt button had popped from its hole. She had to believe he hadn't noticed—but maybe... Flushed with embarrassment, she turned her back to button it.

"You got grass stains on the back of your shirt," George said when she was facing him again.

"It doesn't matter."

"I suppose I should go back to work." George turned to pick up his hoe.

Phyllis was wet from the damp grass. "I suppose I should go back to the house," she said.

●

March, 1940

Beyond her desk, Phyllis saw rag-patches of dirty snow scattered about the yard, but the sun was rising in a clear sky. Soon George would be raking soggy straw from the flower beds. But not yet. Now the winter schedules of school and home held Phyllis in their icy grip, but the frozen seeds in her heart were alive and waiting to escape from the insulation of childhood and the strictures from her mother. Through the summer Phyllis had held to the bonds of propriety. When she saw George, a friendly nod, a *hi,* betrayed no sign of the intensity she was hiding.

Now Phyllis guarded her feelings, only releasing them in her art class with angry images and splashes of warring colors.

She was gazing from her window at two oak leaves swirling in the March wind when Mrs. Dean came into Phyllis's room. "Are you doing your homework, Dear?"

Phyllis picked up a pencil. "Yes." As her mother left the room, she opened the nearest book, the dictionary. She turned to *"Masculine names, George: from Gk.: farmer, worker of the soil."* She knew her name, Phyllis, was Greek too: *"Green leaf."*

Responsibility and guilt dumped into Phyllis's mind, mixed with anger and rebellion, then emerged in a dramatic critique of normal classroom expectations. The history test on Monday: *a time line strung with dates and names, treaties and wars; to me, useless as the skeletons of last year's leaves. Physics, a commanding parent of the universe, ignorant of feeling, decreeing laws that have to be obeyed.* Phyllis's gaze drifted beyond her window to the sunlit day. *Is the melting power of sun only chemistry, its growing power only the motor of photosynthesis, the beauty of it nothing beyond the classical laws of esthetics?*

Phyllis felt a self inside her ready to explode; Arthur would listen, help her make sense of her life. She pushed back her chair and went to him, but not without a guarded reservation about sharing thoughts of George.

"Hi," she said. "Okay if I turn off your radio? It's hard to hear when it's on."

"Yeaa."

"You're lucky you don't read. No one can tell you what to do with your mind." Phyllis looked for his response, then went into his sadness without leaving her own. "But you're lonely?" His head sank down, then jerked up. "But even when it's easy to talk to people, it's hard to make them *really know*."

"Eh."

"Hard to find the words—well—maybe I don't really know myself. Maybe that's why I like to paint, let color talk in a whole pattern at once instead of a line like words."

As he smiled, the lines from his nose to the corners of his mouth rose from their vertical drop. "I—see—that—way."

"Hard, like seeing a flood and telling about it in drops. It's hard. I try to paint—well, I want to paint about love." Her emotions tangled in a mix of allure and fear and a strange *bad*, mixed with bodies, but maybe it was really good. "I only get colors. I can't draw bodies. Like my feelings are stuck inside."

"Tell—me," Arthur said.

"I had this sort-of dream, but I was almost awake. I was seeing a green hill. I could see the exact shape and every shade of color. So clear! Then the bottom seems to spring to life with a great big enormous flock of love birds flying toward me. But one of them looked like a dragon. Blue, with a tooth on the top of its head." Funny, put into words, but Arthur didn't laugh. The sound he made focused raw feeling to Phyllis, inviting her words. "I guess it was because I couldn't paint the movement, just couldn't catch the mood of it. So it turned out just silly."

Arthur was looking out of his window into the limitless

expanse of sky beyond his tree. He seemed to see it. "Ah—wan..."

Phyllis listened to the soft vowels, then guessed, "...to write a story?"

With a tablet on her lap and a pencil in her hand, she waited for his words: "One—time—there—was—a..." Then came two syllables, a short *e* or *i* in the first, an *o* or *u* in the second. The twisting of his face, as he struggled to command his mouth and tongue to form words, indicated a word tight with consonants.

"Child? Indian? Pansy?" For at least ten minutes her guessing went on. Then, in reaction to a fluttering from the windowsill, Arthur swung his arm, pointing with his fist to the violet-breasted bird. "Yes! Pigeon!" she exclaimed.

"One time there was a pigeon," Phyllis read. *"He was very unusual, very pretty. Yellow, red and white. His name was Blue Boy."*

"Blue?" Phyllis questioned. He smiled in answer, and Phyllis tried to respond to his laborious humor.

The labor continued through the morning. Phyllis set down each word exactly as he wished, yet by lunch time they had barely begun; then Phyllis left him feeling sorry that he had to bottle his ideas, awaiting her convenience.

But Arthur had the playmate of his fantasy and the knowledge that he had the means to release it. He forgot the tension that encased him and could feel a limitless life before him. He smiled to his running thoughts.

After lunch the accumulated words tumbled too fast for Phyllis's comprehension. "Cool down," she pleaded.

When Arthur calmed, the work progressed. For nearly a week they labored, Arthur struggling with each word as Phyllis struggled to understand. She transcribed his tale with meticulous accuracy, each scrambled tense and incomplete sentence given as much care as though she were secretary to Moses rendering the ten commandments.

The work was finished. "Now—read." He heard a long string of his own words fast and clear:

"Blue Boy could talk. He lived on a faraway hill in a bird cage. He was lonesome, and he was bored. So he flies over the hill in search of a mate. But it was cloudy. He can't find her. He can't see anything—not until he got to a big hill. It was windy and hard to fly. He worked hard to get over the hill.

"She was sitting in a tree. Blue boy looked all around her because he was too shy to look at her. And then he swoops down upon her!

"He saw branches with green leaves, and he saw her nest. Then he looks at her. She is yellow and red and purple, and she has a pretty pink worm in her beak."

Laughter stopped Phyllis's reading. *"He was going to ask her if she was married. But then he knew. Her mate flew in. He was ugly, and he had a tooth on the top of his head."*

Arthur broke in, "His—name—is—George."

Phyllis ignored the insertion. *"He saw Blue Boy. Blue Boy told him, 'I don't want to fight you.' Then the ugly mate told Blue Boy he could have her, so Blue Boy took her. He asked her what her name was, and it was Mary. They told each other that they loved each other and wanted to be together all the time.*

"Then something happens far away; a baby bird was born. He was an eagle called Flopsy. He was an unusual bird because he couldn't use his wings to fly. He tried to fly the coop, but he couldn't. The other birds didn't accept him because he couldn't fly.

"So one winter day he was just lying in the snow. Blue Boy and Mary found him and they adopted him and took him to their nest."

Arthur pointed to his tree. "The—nest—is—there."

"That baby had some kind of birth defect, and when it flew, it fell hard, so it thought it was a failure. Everybody thought so. Except for one person."

Arthur looked at her hard, and Phyllis felt a greedy pull at her affections: glad for his love, yet resentful of his desire to possess her. It made her feel as though he was attempting to bind her to his chair.

●

It had been unusually warm for March. Phyllis stood in front of her open window pulling on her sweater. When her eyes emerged from the neck, she saw George in the garden below her raking a hopeful welcome to spring rains.

Mrs. Dean's voice filtered through Phyllis's door. "Phyllis, do hurry. Hilda is waiting breakfast." *That schedule, even on Saturday!* Food repelled her, but an argument would be a worse intrusion on her springtime mood. She ate a couple of bites. Her mother's words ran through her without touching... Until...

George. His name riveted Phyllis's attention. "I'm going to have George wash the chandelier today," her mother announced. "The coal dust does get everything so covered with greasy soot!"

Phyllis looked up to the wide dome formed by hundreds of crystal beads strung on wires. Daylight no longer reflected from the crystals tarnished with winter soot.

"Your father and I bought it together, a little antique store in London. It was our wedding trip, almost the only shopping we ever did together. I believe it came from one of the great houses somewhere outside of the city." Her words almost sang, "It will be nice to see it sparkle again, the way it did then."

●

Immediately after lunch Phyllis went down to the basement. She stood in the laundry-room doorway, planning her approach, looking at George. Although his back was partially hidden by a damask tablecloth hanging on the line, he and the chandelier were lit by light from the window that looked out on a sunken porch where snow shovels still leaned against the wall next to the basement door. Phyllis stood in the laundry- room doorway for a long time, but George did not look in her direction. He was drying the chandelier with a dish towel. The south sun sparkled on the polished prisms and made rainbows on the white wall.

She planned to go in pretending to get a clean shirt, then say a casual *Hi*. Although her rubber soles were silent, she felt that her drumming heart must be audible. She approached his back as he bent over the chandelier. "Hi." Her voice too loud! He straightened up with a jerk.

The crash was like roaring thunder with tinkling hail on top of it. "God! No!" George exclaimed.

I'm sorry stuck in Phyllis's throat.

"The thing's heavy. You surprised me."

"I didn't mean to. Really, I'm sorry."

"It's my fault," he said.

"No, it's mine. I'm sorry, really."

He shook his head. "I should have hung on."

They looked at the still-rolling beads of glass, their soft tinkle the only sound.

"I gotta tell her," George said.

"I suppose."

"Will you come too?" George, so strong in everything he did... Now he looked scared. Phyllis nodded.

They halted in front of Mrs. Dean's closed door. Deep, choking sobs struck their ears in explosions with shaking gasps between them. She and George looked at each other in shocked surprise. Then Mrs. Dean seemed to force a shield of control around her voice as she commanded herself, "Stop, stop this weakness. Your family, your family needs you. Arthur, Phyllis..." *John* was covered with choking.

"All this... We shouldn't hear," Phyllis said, yet their feet seemed made of stone until they heard steps inside.

"Maybe she heard us," George hissed.

Phyllis led the way down the hall, and they ducked into Arthur's room.

●

Arthur's door was open, so he could listen to the sounds of the house. From behind his mother's closed door, Arthur heard a shaking noise of hurt or anger. A little while ago his father's voice had come out slowly, something clamped around it. Then he heard his mother's door open, so he could hear his father. "I must live my own life." Later a far-down crash boomed from the basement—the bottom of the house was angry too. Then the front door banged—like an answer. His father getting out.

Ameba-thoughts slithered through the cracks of Arthur's mind. He gave them words: *Father mad, Mother sad. Mad, sad, mad, sad, mad, sad.* He put the words out of his head, put them into the branches of his tree, but the branches talked them back and forth between their twigs. Then wind played with his mother's voice and branches cracked, letting out his father's *mad*. There was a dark place, a hole where a branch had blown away, and Arthur took the words and stuffed them, every one, down the black hole. Then his head felt empty, and he was ready for new thoughts that could carry him outside, far far from the mixed up sounds inside the house. His thoughts did not stay long outside his room.

Arthur heard Phyllis's steps, but George's steps were coming too.

●

Phyllis and George shut Arthur's door. They stood at the top of the ramp.

"What's the matter with her?…Does she know already?"

"How could she?" Phyllis asked.

George shrugged. "I don't know. Maybe she heard the crash when I dropped it. Anybody in the house could hear."

Arthur's head was shaking hard. "I—heard. What—happened?"

"The chandelier, the one in the dining room. It broke," Phyllis said. "We tried to tell Mother, but she was crying. So I felt kind of like a spy or something."

Arthur tried to answer her confusion, "Ah—her…" but Phyllis was not listening.

George swung his arms in unison, forward and back. His thick hands opened, closed; his eyes searched for some thing to hold. "I can't tell her now. What should I do?"

Phyllis shook her head, raked her hair up over her ears.

Arthur jerked his arms hitting the arm of his chair with his right hand. "Ge—ou—o—hee."

"What's all that mean?" George asked.

"He's saying 'Get out of here'." Phyllis glanced sideways at George. "Could we just do that?" She dropped her gaze.

"Yeah." George shrugged. The breadth of his shoulders emphasized the gesture. "Things around here are in a real mess." He turned to Phyllis, ready for action. "Let's go now." He put his hand on the doorknob. Phyllis was torn, wanting to go with George—yet something strange, almost scary about being alone with him now that he was eighteen—a different person. Not just a boy any more.

Arthur was speaking again.

"Wait." Phyllis went to her brother. "We should listen."

"It's—getting—dark."

Phyllis was puzzled. "But the sun is out."

"It—doesn't—matter—how—light—it—gets—if—I—don't—go—outside—the—house."

"You mean you want to come?" Incredulous. Yet his words gave Phyllis a sudden stab of empathy: What would it feel like always to be left behind?

"It—just—might—help—if—I—could—go—out—in—the—world."

"What's all that stuff?" George asked, standing away from Arthur's chair.

"He wants to go with us," Phyllis said.

George muttered an unconvinced "Him?" He looked hard at Phyllis's sympathetic face. "Maybe," he said.

Phyllis felt the lure of forbidden adventure.

"I—go." Determination blazed in Arthur's steady gaze, and his body tightened close to the point of explosion.

Phyllis felt the strength of his desire backed by the threat of a fit of screaming. Now, of all times, she didn't want Arthur's anger exploding on top of her mother's sadness. Her curiosity to know more about her parents' troubles was less than her fear of discovering something really bad going on between them.

Without words, she nodded a decisive *yes*. Immediately afterwards the ever-present *What if we are discovered?* flashed into her mind.

"We gotta do something. Let's go."

George's eagerness sizzled along a fuse to Phyllis. She welcomed the tingle of fear, mixed though it was with awareness of great obstacles. "Let's go," she echoed, standing still.

George spoke in a staccato. "Hurry up. Where's his coat?"

"He never goes out. Even the dentist, he has to come here, to the house. I don't know. I don't know if he even has a coat."

"Then let's you and me just git." George was restlessly shifting from one foot to the other.

Scary; scary to run away with George; guilty to leave Arthur. As she heard Arthur's voice from deep inside him, she said, "We better take him. I said we would."

"Okay, but we gotta wrap him up somehow."

"Yes. A blanket."

"Where?" George looked around the room; he saw and grabbed at the same time, Miss Bitzer's pink blanket for her arthritic knees, folded, laid over the back of her rocker.

Phyllis gripped the back of Arthur's chair with both hands.

"We can't take that chair, too big and noisy," George cautioned as he leaned over Arthur.

"But he's too heavy!"

George had started on a plan of action and ignored Phyllis's hesitation. "Can't weigh much more than a hundred pounds, and I'm real strong." The chair started to roll. "Here, hold this thing steady," George commanded as he unsuccessfully tried to work the blanket around Arthur. "Hey, help get his arm down, will you?"

Phyllis leaned down to set the brake, then took Arthur's arm: rigid, brittle; it felt as though it would snap. "Try to relax."

Phyllis kept her downward pressure gentle. They waited. Little by little the spasticity eased until Phyllis could press the arm down to his side.

"Okay." George lifted Arthur from his chair, and Phyllis pulled the blanket under him, wrapped his arms to his sides.

"Looks like a big baby," George said looking down at the swaddled bundle in his arms.

Phyllis saw Arthur tighten against the word, but George walked up the ramp, oblivious. Phyllis ran ahead, opened the door. The whole house, like a cat at a mouse hole, seemed to be waiting. "I guess we can go," Phyllis whispered.

They walked along the hall. George's breath sounded too loud, his steps too heavy. He turned left toward the backstairs. "No, this way," Phyllis whispered.

"How come?"

Why does he have to be so loud?

"My coat." Phyllis led the way down the front stairs to the closet.

"My jacket's in the basement."

Why can't he whisper. "You stay back here," she said. George stood against the wall behind the kitchen door as Phyllis opened it. Dishes clattered from the pantry, but otherwise the kitchen was quiet. Phyllis signaled, and George followed. A knock against the door jamb; it was Arthur's hand. His arm had thrust out from the blanket. No time to coax it back. Phyllis tiptoed through the kitchen, but George, with Arthur's weight and his leather-soled boots could not tread quietly. Phyllis held her breath until they reached the door to the basement, then down the stairs that didn't squeak.

In the basement Phyllis began to relax.

"I guess we made it," George said. They walked easily toward the laundry room. "My jacket's on the ironing board."

George set his pink burden on the table, with Phyllis's hand to steady Arthur, and went for his jacket.

"I—wan—one."

Phyllis followed the direction of Arthur's eyes. One clear

bead sparkled in the center of the floor. "I'll get it." Phyllis opened his clenched fingers and put the bead in his hand.

"Pretty." Only a tiny facet of it showed, but it caught the sunlight, a point of white, then turning red.

"I guess we better go," George said. He didn't take time to zip his leather jacket, so when he bent over Arthur, the jacket tented above him.

"You better zip your jacket first," Phyllis said.

"Naw. I don't like to get hot." But when he straightened up, the zipper flapped against Arthur's head, and he dropped the crystal. Phyllis picked it up and put it in her pocket.

They went into the yard where wind blew away the closeness of the house. "Wheeoo!" George exclaimed.

Arthur's lungs opened, snatching at the sharp air. "I—glad—" He looked up at George, "—almost."

Phyllis smiled back at him, then questioned George. "Where should we go?"

George led her beside the garage, then down a narrow stairway that was dug into the hillside and supported by a concrete retaining wall. Over the top was a trellis covered with vines, dead-looking sticks waiting for spring leaves. The passage felt like a culvert. "Nobody can see us from the house," he said. Above them only the third-floor windows and the slate roof were visible through the vines overhead. "Hurry up," he urged. With Arthur angular in his arms, George was standing ahead of Phyllis outside the arched gate at the bottom of the steps. They could see down over the succession of terraces that would soon be blooming with flowers. Now the beds were muddy where they were not mulched with straw. George stopped and attempted to adjust the blanket and shift Arthur's weight closer against his chest. "He ain't so heavy, but he's real hard to hold with all that jerking." Arthur reacted to George's comment with another spastic contraction. "I guess it'll be okay now. We're almost there."

Wondering where *there* was, Phyllis followed along a path against the hill where a few lingering patches of snow sent their chill up around her ankles. The wind had turned icy in spite of the protection of the hill. With every step, Phyllis felt more and more that their whole idea was a mistake. Yet she followed with her fear balanced equally between turning back or going forward.

"Arthur, are you cold?" she asked. But she could not tell whether the sound he made was *yes* or *no*.

"Here." George opened a little door in the wall supporting the bank above which the garage was built, and they looked into the dark interior of a garden shed. The walls were of limestone pressed into the clay of the bank, and everything inside was diminutive except for George bent double over the pink-wrapped Arthur. He stepped through the door into the low-ceilinged room with rakes, spades, forks and stakes in the corner. Pots, trowels, flats and packages of seeds were on the rough wood shelves. In the diminutive surroundings, Phyllis felt her childhood around her, as though transplanted into the house of a small animal from the pages of Beatrix Potter.

Out of the wind, they felt warmer. "Come on."

"Where?" she asked. With his foot, George indicated a pile of nested bushel baskets. "Can you move this stuff?"

Phyllis pulled the baskets back uncovering a narrow, cave-like tunnel. "I never knew this was here!"

"Nobody knows. Just me. It's a real limestone cave I guess. Come on, we're going through."

"Will it cave in? With the garage on top of it?"

"Naw. It's been here forever. They got concrete footings under that garage would hold up a skyscraper."

"Can you crawl with Arthur?"

"Naw. We'll leave him here."

For a moment Phyllis watched with her mouth gaping in disbelief as George kicked some scattered burlap bags into a pile. She realized he intended to put Arthur on top of them. He reacted with a spastic jerk that shuddered George's entire body.

"No!" Phyllis exclaimed.

George took a step backward and almost dropped Arthur as

he heard the force of her horrified explosion. "I figured…" he began. "I just…I wanted to show you something real pretty…" His action aborted, he stood as still as he could against Arthur's spastic thrusts.

"But why can't Arthur come too?"

"I kind of thought it would be just us."

"But don't you see? It's Arthur too! It was his idea too."

"It'll be real hard to get him there." George looked down at the burden in his arms, motion without direction and sound without meaning. He looked up at Phyllis in silent confusion; then Phyllis could see, not his cruelty, but his ignorance.

Although Arthur was trying to speak, he was too upset to be understood.

"We won't leave you. George didn't understand what you wanted. But…" Phyllis looked up at George, "Why did you say he could come?"

"I don't know. I thought you'd like it. I didn't know he'd be…" Phyllis was glad to see him look down at Arthur without saying what she guessed he was thinking.

"Inside he's not so different from us. He wants to do what we do." Arthur made confirming sounds.

As he looked down at Arthur, George's expression slowly transformed from a cold look at a troublesome armload of jerks to registering, at least a little regard for a feeling person. "Okay, fellow. We'll get you through this somehow."

"Aahh." Arthur understood George's change of attitude, and Phyllis managed to put him back on the pedestal she had constructed for him in her heart.

The tunnel was narrow, and the floor was slicked by ice. George layered three burlap bags, lifted Arthur onto them and used them like the net of a hammock to hold Arthur off the ground as they pulled him, as gently as they could, over the slick floor of the passage. George led, Phyllis crawled behind holding Arthur's feet and trying, not very successfully, to keep the burlap under him while guiding his stockinged feet so that they did not catch on the limestone thrusting from the sides of the tunnel. The ground, ice-hard, ice-cold, penetrated Phyllis's corduroy slacks and stiffened her fingers as they groped forward into the dark tunnel. But there was a warmth about it too, the sound of scuffing dirt and Arthur's excited laughter echoing from the sides of the tunnel as he relished even the discomfort of his first adventure. Ahead of her, Phyllis heard George's heavy breathing blending with her own.

"We're here," George said as light brightened the opening space ahead of them. Arthur gasped in wonder.

"Real pretty, ain't it?" George stood, leaning Arthur against the wall and bracing him with his leg. He offered Phyllis his hand which, framed in a halo of light, did not seem real enough to touch. Phyllis looked to the space beyond. Just one shaft of sunlight in the tiny room, but it slanted over a wall of ice turning it to shimmering light. "Enter my diamond castle." He pulled her up, and she stood beside him with Arthur pressed between them. Phyllis looked up at George's face, dark against the light, framed as his hand was framed with an eerie underground sun. Her hand remained in George's: big, rough, warm. "You're cold," he said.

"I guess so." Phyllis felt Arthur move, heard him start to speak. "You must be cold too," she said, leaning over to see his face as he answered.

"I—fine."

"Really? Oh good."

"I—almost—alone."

"Do you want to be alone? You mean without Miss Bitzer or Mother?"

"Without—them."

George helped Phyllis move Arthur to a corner of the room and tuck the blanket tight around him. "But you won't be alone here. This room is too small."

"Aahh." The corner of the earth wall gave him some support, and he faced the glittering display.

"I'm glad you're here," Phyllis said.

"My—aah." Phyllis didn't get the word, but it might be *Idea*.

George took her hand and pulled her back and away from Arthur's view. "Look," he was unzipping his jacket, "there's room for both of us." The flannel lining across her back was warm from his body. The ice outside, the fire within; she shivered between the two. "Warmer now?" he asked. Her head pressed against his chest, and his heat flowed through her. "I know we're under the garage, but the light is a mystery," he said.

Phyllis wanted to tell him. She tried. "I had a dream last night."

"This is a good place for dreams." His voice changed, low and soft. His breath was warm; his lips touched her ear.

"Shh. Arthur," she said.

Phyllis felt the light and lavender of her dream pouring through her body to the earth. "Yes. This place…It's like a picture of, I mean it makes my dream seem real."

"Yeah. And you…real things seem like a dream." His arms pulled her tighter, and she was aware of his strength becoming almost part of her own body.

Then a voice out of the earth, exploding loud…George's arms jerked Phyllis close, pulling so hard it almost hurt. "What's the matter with him?"

Phyllis felt a mix of shame and guilt as she looked at Arthur. "He fell over," she said, breaking away from George, feeling the damp air between them.

Arthur's pink blanket was incongruously scrambled with the burlap sacks. "I'm sorry, I didn't see you tip over." Phyllis squatted beside him and pulled the blanket around his body. When he was quiet again, Phyllis saw his eyes roll up. She followed his glance to the icicles hanging from the ceiling, their edges shined by light, and she broke off one for him to feel. When she put it in his hand, it slipped down to shatter on the floor of the cave.

"Didn't you know how cold it would be?"

"The—sun—on—it," he said.

"But it's just like ice in a glass. It's *cold,* and you're cold too." She turned to Geroge. "We'd better go now. Arthur's really cold."

George pulled Phyllis up and drew her close against his chest. "So soon?"

"Yes, we have to go." She pulled away from him and took one last look at the beauty of the cave. "Thank you for bringing me to this magic place—and it didn't cave in."

"Told you it wouldn't." He held her hand. "It was hard to get here, but I'm glad you liked it."

They entered the dark tunnel. Phyllis kept the beauty in her center as she laboriously crawled after the dim forms of George and Arthur, back to the potting shed. "Where we were was so beautiful! Like the whole world was made of light."

"...instead of crud from Pa washing the car."

"What!?"

George was grinning at her. "That place drains the garage, sort of a sewer-like."

"No!"

He stepped back from her disgust. "It's not the real dirty stuff."

George scooped up Arthur's frail body and they went, blinking, into the sun.

Phyllis asked Arthur, "Are you getting warmer?"

He threw back silence like a stone.

George spoke to her softly, "I don't want to take you back." Then, in the narrow passage under the arch below the steps, he backed Phyllis against the wall and looked above Arthur as if he were invisible. "You're real pretty." She felt Arthur's spastic thrusts through the length of her body as George pressed him sandwiched between them. Her heart pounded with the strength of all her emotions at once. She looked up at George feeling helpless as a butterfly caught in a gush of water down a drainpipe. He leaned over her, but she suddenly ducked her head in embarrassed confusion. His kiss reached only her hair. He stepped back as Phyllis muttered, "No."

Arthur's spear of words found no understanding. His body nearly jerked from George's arms.

Each gripped in their own tension, they reached the back

door. George clamped his hand over Arthur's mouth. "You gotta shut up."

A roar of hurt escaped from his locked up body. Fighting George and his own disobedient muscles, his hand jutted out against the wall of the back stairwell, scraping the skin from his knuckles.

George's frustration exploded. "For godsake quit fighting. Are you crazy?"

Arthur's body quivered against George's grip, struggled against his muscles, while quiet order filled the air around them: the regular hum of basement motors, the distant rumble of the vacuum cleaner, the clink of dishes from the kitchen.

George labored up the back-hall steps with Arthur, took him to his room and put him roughly in his chair. He hurried away without speaking.

Arthur's body still shivered, and his mind felt scrambled and smeared like the pink blanket thrown over the back of Miss Bitzer's chair. He stared at the mud stains, then at the fresh blood on the satin binding of the corner.

●

In the kitchen Phyllis greeted Hilda casually while her heart raced. Had anyone been in Arthur's room while they were gone? Phyllis knew Miss Bitzer had a cold again, but Mother? She would not have gone into Arthur's room when she was upset. Yet maybe...

Helen was peeling potatoes. "Can you take Arthur's tray? I'm real busy."

"Yes. But where's Mother?"

"Still in her room for all I know, and Miss Bitzer's got that cold." Phyllis could feel Hilda's, *she's no help anyway.*

Phyllis poured Arthur's milk. "Then nobody's with Arthur?" she asked, taking off her coat and tossing it onto a chair.

"It won't hurt him to be alone once in awhile. After all, I can't do everything."

"Of course not." Phyllis had forgotten it was lunch time; such good luck that they were back in time. She took the tray.

"You can feed him, can't you?" Hilda's irritation followed Phyllis up the back stairs. "I suppose you want me to hang up your coat."

"That's all right. I'll do it later."

"I'm sorry. Your mother was in a bad mood, and I…" Hilda checked her sentence.

"I don't mind," Phyllis called down from the steps. With her secret safe, she felt no inclination to object to Hilda's irritated barbs. "I know you've got a lot to do, and now with all Miss Bitzer's toothaches and stomach upsets, you have to fix special food for her too."

As she went down the ramp, the pink blanket stained with evidence drew her attention. "I've got to get this out of here." Hurriedly Phyllis put down Arthur's tray and took the blanket to the clothes chute. When she returned, he was hunched in his chair. He looked smaller than usual. She held out a spoonful of meat loaf, but Arthur compressed his lips. "All right if I eat it then?"

The movement of his eyes showed permission without forgiveness.

Phyllis bent over the tray, the black one with a gold dragon spitting fire. Glowing gold—gold that reminded her of their shining ice palace… Arthur's voice pulled her from her thoughts. "What?" she mumbled, her mouth full.

He repeated, "My—diamond?"

"Yes, your crystal, I have it." She took it from her pocket and handed it to him.

"I—want—to—write—something."

"Really? I thought you were too mad at me." Phyllis got the notebook.

It didn't take long:

"Dear Mary,
Your boyfriend is a dragon. I want you to come and see

me because you are my friend. I have a diamond for you.
Love, Arthur"

"But you don't know any Mary."

"She—came." Arthur's face was clenched in defiance. He dropped his crystal, wanted Phyllis to pick it up. He would only drop it again and again; she wanted only to be by herself. He screamed after her as she left, his crystal beyond his reach.

Phyllis went into the bathroom, filled the tub. Just to be undisturbed. She stretched in the warm water, watched little prisms of crystal falling from the dripping spout: lost. Another drop growing. With just a little help from her mind, the drop swelled big enough to hold an image of George. She closed her eyes. Smooth round drop, its yellow edging made his hair, blue eyes looking out at her *naked* body. She looked down at her breasts. So big! It was George's eyes that transformed her familiar body, put it in the center of a new world. Her breathing stirred the water over her nipples giving them movement like pebbles in a clear stream. Her navel, a hidden place, like a hole in the ground when it's covered with snow; can't tell how deep it is. Hair between her legs bubbled with tiny beads of air. Another drop swelling, quickly falling. Beads of water in the air, beads of air in the water, water in the air, air in the water. Drop following drop following drop. She pulled the washcloth over her breasts. The bubbles rose from the troubled water in little chains from her pubic hair leaving a naked black tuft between her legs that hid a place still scarcely known, a deep place in a valley guarded by hills, a hard little lump she had quickly felt, but never seen; like the fruit of the tree of knowledge, never to be touched. Phyllis remembered her childhood baths.... Miss Bitzer? her mother? instructing her: "First we wash up as far as possible, then we wash down as far as possible..." (Yes, it was Miss Bitzer.) Phyllis could see her coy smile as she handed over the soapy washcloth saying, "Then we wash Possible." That must have been her raciest joke.

Phyllis focused on another drop, a tear that illustrated Arthur's voice as it intruded through the locked door. Mother crying... That mother and that father: how had they ever had a baby? How could I come to be?

The dripping faucet lulled away her questions, moved her into dream-time. ...a craggy beach strewn with stones. It seemed important to throw them out over the vast water, do it with George's smooth strength. She picked up one that looked like a miniature mountain. She clutched it, drew her arm back, then pushed with all her strength. But, like Arthur's, her hand did not open as she threw, and the stone dropped at her feet.

●

The next morning Phyllis was walking toward her room with a glass of orange juice in her hand.

"I told her." George's voice grated through his whisper.

"You surprised me!" A blackening splash of juice was dribbling down her blue skirt.

"I just told her."

"About the chandelier?"

"Yeah," George said.

"How did she take it?"

"She got real quiet and kinda looked away, but she didn't fly off ner nothing. She said she'd get it fixed. I don't know how with so many of them crystals broke. But I didn't ask her nothing. I just got out of there real quick."

Phyllis brushed at the orange juice as her mind brushed at George's rough grammar. It was hard for him when his parents spoke with such a heavy accent, and probably the kids at his school all talked the same way. But he could learn when he heard it right.

His wrists were thick and strong between his fanning hands and the short cuffs of his blue work shirt. Like the practicing wings of a young hawk, his fingers opened and closed.

"I wanna ask you something." The new softness in his voice drew a matching softness in her heart. "I wana see you. Can you get out tonight? We could kinda walk around."

She nodded. Later she would figure out how.

●

Dinner took intolerably long, but finally desert was finished, and Phyllis bolted upstairs. She went into her room to comb her hair with water, try to smooth it down, and put on her lipstick.

When she heard her mother's steps in the hall, she shouted through the door, struggling to sound casual. "I'm going out."

Phyllis heard the dreaded answer. "It is too late to go outside."

A few seconds later a key grated in the lock of her door.

"It's my door, my key!" she shouted.

Trapped fury kept her raw and hurting. She buried her face in her pillow and cried. Hate, rage, pain, love: they wrapped Phyllis in tangled threads and pulled her tight.

She heard her father shouting, commanding: "Deirdre, you must let Phyllis out! This is 1940. The Victorian age is past. You're acting like your *father's* wife. Just because you were brought up in an ideological straitjacket, you don't have to inflict the same restraints on Phyllis. Aren't you in touch at all?"

"It is unfair for you to attack my age. I did not choose to be forty three when Phyllis was born."

"Phyllis is fourteen years old, and it's *her* age that matters now. You do not have the right to lock the door on her life."

"Yes, she is *only* fourteen and much too young and vulnerable to go out alone at night. I shall do everything I can to keep her safe."

Her father continued in a quieter voice. "Deirdre, how is she going to learn to take care of herself and make her own decisions if we never give her a chance to make any? Yes, there are dangers in life, but all of us must learn to face them in our own way."

"John, you know there could be prowlers about, and a young girl is completely defenseless."

"Yes, and a meteor could tumble out of the sky or she could be in an automobile accident on her way to school."

"You know how important our children are to me. The center of my life is their welfare."

"Yes, I know you do your very best, but regulating everything in their physical and mental surroundings is no way to teach them to become self-directing adults. Believe me, living in a dictatorship, no matter how benevolent, is no way to teach Phyllis to become a mature adult. Did your father's constant demands on your life give you courage to move out in a world of emancipated women?"

"Do *not* bring my father into it. He did his very best to be both mother and father to me. He hired the very best refined people he could find, and saw to it that I learned careful diction and good manners and fine taste, he..."

Her father interrupted. "This is another age. Please give me that key."

Phyllis heard her father's tread, then the click of the lock as she listened to him say, "This house is the danger. Not the outside world." His words were followed by his retreating steps, then Phyllis heard the front door slam as she rushed out of her room and down the back stairs.

Juliet flashed to Phyllis's mind as she slipped out of the kitchen door, away from conflict. The air was sharp and cold. She sensed George close before she saw him walking from the shadow of the blue spruce.

"The snow's mostly gone," he said.

They walked without touching. Phyllis interrupted the silence, loud with emotion. "It's good to feel the ground getting soft—in spots."

"Almost time for baseball."

Down below Crest Parkway they stood beside a vacant lot. Shadowy houses formed a semicircle around the black ground. "This is where we play ball when the mud sort of dries up."

As they walked back toward the house, the stars came close salting them with light. Standing by the spruce, George was bending over Phyllis. His lips brushed her forehead, then came back to her eyebrow and stayed for a long time.

"Oh, George," she gasped.

His arms circled her. As she rested her face against him, she felt the rough cloth of his work shirt, smelled its soap-clean smell, and underneath it his heartbeat, strong, against her cheek. She hoped so much, then really believed their love could hold them this close forever. In a comforting way his strength was hers, a protection from the dictates of her mother. So close against him—she felt their bodies blend, tying her to his strength. She lifted her face, wanting his lips on hers, wanting to hear him say *I love you*.

Instead, the shrill call of her mother's voice—"Phyllis. Phyllis. It's time to come in."

They froze.

The call came once again. The spell was broken.

"I better go in."

"I suppose so," he said.

●

His kiss was still touching her two weeks later on March 27, the morning of her fifteenth birthday. The smell of coffee wafted from the dining room. It was Saturday, a baseball game, and she would be *with George all afternoon.*

Her mother's sing-song call gave—to Phyllis—a false tug at cheerfulness that halted her reverie. "Surprise!" A curtain had shrouded her mother for two weeks, but now her tone was jubilant. "Phyllis, your grandfather is coming clear from Boston for your birthday party. And right now Carl has left for the station to meet his train. He will be here for dinner, and I hired some help for Hilda, so everything will go smoothly."

"Sunday dinner!" It would take forever. The afternoon she

had awaited for nearly a month was threatened. Replacing her joyful expectations, her grandfather swelled in her mind: big black vest looped by a gold watch chain. Behind the vest the voice that rumbled out, holding forth forever, talking for itself with only her mother listening.

With the same eager cheerfulness her mother exclaimed, "Happy birthday, Dear Child!"

Phyllis pulled away from her mother's infantilizing words followed by an unwelcome embrace. "Not again! Will you stop calling me that!"

"You grow up too fast! Sometimes I…" Arthur's distant voice interrupted her. "I wonder what he wants."

"I'll go." Phyllis had avoided speaking to Arthur about George, but that did not check Arthur's resentment or his clinging look that Phyllis felt as an incessant pull whenever she was with him.

Miss Bitzer, moving more quickly than she normally did, stood up as Phyllis walked down the ramp. "I can't understand a word he says!" She had a pad of paper in her hand which she held toward Phyllis. "He wants me to write something. Maybe your young ears can figure it out." She walked up the ramp, the wispy bun at the back of her neck vibrating with impatience and incoherent words mumbling from her lips.

Arthur's head was thrown back, his mouth open as though his jaw had no hinges. The resulting tension corded his neck, and Phyllis went to him, listening to his choking voice. She put her hand on the back of his head, waiting, waiting, until his head eased forward.

"I—get—lonesome."

"I'm sorry."

"You—don't—come."

"I've been busy."

"George?" he asked.

Phyllis shrugged off the question. "I hardly ever see him."

"He—doesn't—like—me."

"He doesn't know you."

"He—doesn't—listen. He—doesn't—try."

Phyllis stood, wanting to leave, but Arthur wouldn't let her.

"Happy—birthday."

"Thanks."

"I—want—to…" Phyllis shook her head at the last word. "—give. Give—you—something." She nodded. "I—want—to—write—something. For—you."

As he dictated, Phyllis thought of a stone tongue chipping at words, trying to make freedom.

> *YOU HEAR ME*
> *Young lad sits inside, walls all around him.*
> *That lad, he wants beauty in his life, snow gone*
> *The world outside, blue and white sky*
> *Bright green grass, flowers that smell like the rain in spring*
> *Alone in the wild life, tall tall trees, calm and free.*
> *Sister, hear me*
> *I am all closed up inside*
> *I want someone open up my fear*
> *My life is passing by me*
> *I try to hold on tight*
> *I don't want somebody to take the only life I have.*

Phyllis stroked the paper. "Thank you." Her love churned with guilt and regret, and tears started out of the conflict.

They stopped with her mother's call. "Phyllis, do come down stairs. Your grandfather has arrived!"

Phyllis stroked Arthur's shoulder, then reluctantly left the room. She put Arthur's poem on her desk and pulled on the yellow dress her mother bought without consulting her. This year she could not ask for her cake in Arthur's room which was too small, too informal, and the steps would be too much for her grandfather. When his daughter married, his age had already left him puffing at the top of the steps. So he gave up the house and moved to "my" Boston.

Slowly Phyllis went toward her grandfather. He belonged in

the front hall as solidly as the dark oak furniture, the chairs that no one sat on. The gold links that looped across his vest started and ended somewhere out of sight—what his insides were made of? She smiled; Arthur would laugh at Grandfather's solid-gold guts. Sometime she would tell George.

"Well, well, well, so this is our little Phyllis."

She dutifully presented her cheek for his damp kiss. "Now let me take a look at you." He took her shoulders and held her at arms length. "Such a sweet dress, my dear. Brand-new for your special day."

Her father came down the stairs, and Phyllis happily stepped back from central attention as he greeted his father–in–law. She trailed them all as Mr. Dean led the way into the living room. She observed his back, knowing that his face would be set with the same resignation as his shoulders.

Mrs. Dean took her father's arm, leaned toward him and turned her face to his. "My girl must put away these sighs," her father responded. "Difficult times pass by." His daughter obeyed with extra height in every step and a girlish toss to her head.

They sat, and the Voice went on with the lulling cadences of a minister preaching in a foreign language. Only now and then a phrase came clear, "However, my dear Deirdre, the Roosevelt administration is meddling in every phase of our free enterprise system." Phyllis gazed at the marble clock on the marble mantle and watched the minute hand creep invisibly toward twelve.

"Insomuch as the superior earning power...injustices of corporate taxation, Deirdre my dear..."

The watched clock warning of fleeting time, began to strike. Thinking of baseball, Phyllis counted, *strike one.*

"Dinner is served," Hilda announced. Phyllis's mother led; only four of them, but moving toward the dining room with the slowness of a long procession.

Dinner, with the endlessness of watching while her grandfather's fork waved in mid-air marking time between his words.

Her mother's laugh was stagy. "Oh, but you do cut to the center of things! I've always said there is nothing sharper than a keen legal mind."

Mr. Dean poised his knife over the ham shank. "But for meat I prefer high-carbon steel. Would anyone like another slice of ham?" No one had finished their first helping. He winked at Phyllis and smiled, his expression exaggerated like a toothbrush ad.

Phyllis watched the fanning of the swinging door as the plates were removed.

"And now, my little yellow butterfly…" Her grandfather was patting his hard-stuffed vest, lifting his heavy face into a smile, "The awaited moment. I hope your bellows are in good form for blowing out those birthday candles—fifteen is it?"

Mrs. Dean's laugh trilled a solo. "My Phyllis fifteen! Now isn't this a happy occasion?"

Hilda brought the cake; Phyllis blew out the day-pale flames. Next, presents. She tore through the wrappings: watch from her mother; a dress, supposed to be from Arthur, but her mother's idea and selected by her. From her father, *Exploring the Canadian Arctic*, the cover blue and white with ice and snow while tulips and jonquils in their garden were preparing to push through the soggy ground, and the first fuzzy flowers of crocuses were blooming. "Thanks a lot." The silence waited for more. "When I read it, I'll think of you there."

"It's quite a place. Perhaps I'll show it to you someday."

"Fun," she answered. Her eyes were on the clock. Already two thirty-five, and coffee still to come. Phyllis knew how her grandfather's thick fingers would squeeze around the handle of that little cup, on and on into the afternoon.

She just had to go! "Excuse me," she mumbled. She slid around her chair and darted from the room, against her mother's thoughts calling her back.

She did not feel safe until she pulled the heavy door closed and stood on the front step. *But my clothes!* White sandals and a childish dress of yellow dotted swiss!

Back through the kitchen toward her room, passing Hilda in front of the sink with her hands deep in soap suds, not looking up. Phyllis ducked into the back hall, ran up the stairs two at a time. Grabbing from her closet, shirt, jeans, tennis shoes, no time for socks. Then running—straight to where her mother stood blocking the route to either stairway.

"Phyllis, my dear, do come downstairs. Your grandfather has something wonderful to tell you." At least she made no comment on Phyllis's clothes.

"Your grandfather has come all the way from Boston with a wonderful present for you. You simply cannot keep him waiting."

She must follow her mother down the stairs. Light came between the spindles of the banister casting shadows that striped the gray of her mother's dress with prison bars.

Her grandfather stood by the fireplace, his right arm on the mantle, finger hooked into his cup handle, pipe resting in the ash tray. She watched the two blue ribbons of smoke, one from each nostril, then blurring together. Praying: *Please, for once just let him say it and be done!*

"Well, well, well. Our little lady is fifteen. And how many years of high school do you have remaining?"

"Three. I'm going to be a sophomore."

"Well now, that is not very long, is it?" His watch chain straightened when he took a breath.

"No." The expected answer, but three years seemed forever.

"Now then, it isn't a bit too early to start planning for the future, is it?"

"No."

"I suppose that you have been doing a great deal of thinking about college." He had not quite asked a question, so, although he paused, she avoided giving him an answer that would be a lie. "Now your mother never had such an opportunity, and it will mean so much to her to see you matriculated in a fine college. Perhaps Smith or Vassar?"

"Well, I..." It would not do to tell him she planned to go to art school.

"However, there will be problems. Your mother tells me that your scholastic record is not as good as it might be."

Phyllis looked out of the window at the plump buds on the maple.

"Only able scholars are matriculated in institutions like Smith and Vassar. That means that you will have to apply yourself with real vigor."

The clock. Phyllis moved her lips, counting: *strike one, strike two, strike three.* The drone of his modulated voice was a background Phyllis pushed aside; she saw an image of George's straight hair stuck in a point to the sweat of his forehead as...

"Phyllis! Say *thank you* to your grandfather."

Her "Thank you" was a rote response. *Love*—It mattered so much that nothing else mattered at all, and the word, *tuition*, disappeared behind emotion's compelling pull.

"Well, I should hope so!" Embarrassment distorted her mother's laughter. "Not every girl gets four years of college tuition for her birthday."

Phyllis stretched her mouth into a smile.

"Now let's sit down and talk to Grandfather." Her mother patted the sofa beside her. Phyllis sat on the edge, her legs tense, feet pressing the floor.

"A pleasant afternoon with my two favorite girls. What could be finer?" The sun was sinking lower.

"I've told Phyllis so often about the wonderful afternoons we had in your study. I regret so much that she was not there to share our pleasant times."

"You were always a fine listener, my dear Deirdre. I'm afraid the books I selected were often over your head, but you were never the frivolous one. I could not have expected that—after the tragic loss of your mother. I hope you realize, Phyllis, how fortunate you are?"

"I know."

"I am certain you do!" He stood up.

Tense to spring, Phyllis's legs trembled, but her grandfather's hand came heavily to her shoulder. "Now I call this a perfect afternoon for motoring! Spring, and all the dicky birds are singing." Then his flat voice hit the lines of "The Mikado" like the feet of a trampling elephant: *"The flowers that bloom in the spring, tra la..."*

Her escape too late, Phyllis walked slowly down the hill. The wind blew cloud tatters across the crescent moon.

The baseball diamond was full of ghosts, home plate a board weathered pale, cracked like a broken tombstone; second base was an old rag fluttering purple-blue in the moonlight. A grave-yard for the whole afternoon.

Phyllis saw her way back up the hill through tears.

Outside the bone-gray of her house she lingered, staring at shadows until she made them form a shape of George. Really? standing by that bush? or was it the ghost of hope?

She saw him move, heard his "Hi."

"Hi." She said it twice, the first attempt was only breath.

"I didn't think you'd come out."

"I didn't think you'd be here."

"A good birthday party?"

"I don't know," she mumbled. "It was so long, and I wanted to get out. How did you know it was my birthday?"

"My pa."

"Oh."

Around the hedge and down the hill, and then they walked where Phyllis had not been before. Low piles of stone slabs with tall weeds growing around them standing graceful, tall as giraffes. Phyllis dissected her thought, then decided it was too bizarre to voice. "Oh, George," she whispered.

He stopped. "Sky's real blue tonight, ain't it?"

She looked up at the sky and saw purple-black. "Yes, blue," she agreed.

"Stare you down," he said, jerking her out of the feather-soft mood she floated in.

As Phyllis met his eyes, he pushed a sharp-edged package into her hands. "Happy birthday." He laughed as she had to look down.

"See? Told you I could stare you down.... Had to find a dark place 'cause I wrapped it real messy."

She tore away the paper, watched it blow to the ground like the wing of a giant butterfly as she murmured, "Thank you." Phyllis opened the box to the dark inside.

"Kind of hard to see. Anyhow, it's a necklace," he said.

"I can see—sort of."

"Yaw, it's real dark out. Want me to put it on for you?" Phyllis felt the rough hands she knew, as a gentle tickle on the back of her neck. His breath, smelling of peppermint toothpaste, stirred the hair over her ear. He stepped in front of her. "I guess it looks real nice. Sort of like our diamond castle." His eyes drew light from the near-dark so that they looked like giant pearls with jet centers. He held her, and the naked nerve of her heart was tight against him. She clutched, afraid of the inevitable slip of time. He kissed her—right on the lips, and for a long time she looked at the dark of his eyelids and the darker new moon curve of his eyelash. She did not dare close her eyes and risk shutting out the reality.

"Jeez but I love you." The breath of his words caressed her cheek as the electrified current of their meaning surged through her. That she was the recipient of all that love was beyond belief, yet she believed him totally.

"I love you too." They had both said it. Those sacred words meant forever.

They walked for a long, silent time. The breeze left the leaves, and they hung black and still against the sky. They sat on the garden bench, holding each other in a tight embrace. "I'm almost scared," Phyllis said.

"How come?"

"It's so perfect." Phyllis thought of a swallowtail butterfly, it's delicate wings too fragile to withstand the bleaching sun and ripping winds of the world. "Sort of like a butterfly," she said, "so beautiful but only alive for a few days."

"We ain't butterflies," he said.

She laughed, but only a little; his voice was grating. She looked up at his square face. Love and darkness together softened the crags of it. They kissed, and her fears dissipated.

In the end, she had to say it, "I guess I have to go home—but it feels like home with you." Their steps became slower and slower as they approached the back door. Before she put her hand on the doorknob, his lips, full and soft, pressed against hers one more time.

The door was locked. Phyllis had to ring the bell. The opening of the door jarred against her ears.

"My Dear, where have you been? So long! I was really worried."

"I just walked around," she said. "It was beautiful out. I sat on the bench in the garden for a long time."

"You were out for a *very* long time."

"It didn't seem long at all," she said, following her Mother toward the living room.

Her grandfather was gone. Her father was sitting in his chair reading, a circle of lamp-light spilling into his lap. When her mother switched on the overhead light, he became part of the room, and Phyllis didn't notice him any more.

Her mother turned toward her as Phyllis blinked in the bright light.

"Phyllis!"

She saw her mother's eyes focused on her neck, then clamped her hands protectively over her sparkling necklace.

"Where did you get that?" she asked in a carefully controlled voice. Her eyes fixed Phyllis, compelling an answer.

"George," she blurted out. "He gave it to me for my birthday." Phyllis returned her mother's gaze, challenging her to say what she thought: *red, white and blue glass; such common taste!*

Her mother opened her mouth, closed it again, and they continued to stare into each other's eyes. When her mother spoke, the lines between her eyebrows showed her worry, but her words passed her tight lips with polite control. "How nice."

Her father got up from his chair and walked over to her.

"That was a thoughtful thing for him to do," he said.

"Perhaps not altogether appropriate," her mother said.

"I like it," Phyllis answered. "Now it's late, and I'm going to bed."

Before she went to sleep, Phyllis repeated over and over, *he kissed me. Right on the mouth.*

IV

December, 1941

It was snowing and the wind was blowing violently. By contrast, the Sunday hush in Arthur's room seemed even more pervasive than usual. In warm security, Phyllis found it easy to slow down to Arthur's tempo.

"I—am—so—glad—you—come—I—get—bored."

Phyllis looked out at the feather-flakes of snow blowing horizontally, clouding the air, to Phyllis's eyes, hypnotic.

"I—am—tired—of—being—a—monotonous—person." Arthur watched the snow. "I—turn—into—the—pour—of—a—river—in—winter."

"I don't understand—*pour?*—Do you mean like a frozen waterfall? Your muscles feel frozen?"

Arthur shook his head; his eyes agreed with Phyllis. "All—of—me—like—that."

"I know *f* is hard, but next time try saying *fall*."

"The—snow—is—*falling*—quietly."—They exchanged a smile, then looked back to the storm. Only the feathery oak twigs that nearly brushed the window glass were visible, the parent trunk obscured by gusts of blowing snow. Behind their glass shield they felt a warm windless peace. "As if snow drowns the whole world in silence," Phyllis said. From a distant room came indistinguishable words from a radio. That was peaceful too.

Suddenly, "Phyllis!" Their mother was standing in the doorway. "I have just heard shocking news over the radio." Her face was painted with disaster. "The Japanese have bombed Pearl Harbor."

"The Japanese!" They paint cherry blossoms on fans and make little pearls of paper that open into flowers when you drop them in a glass of water. "Where's Pearl Harbor?"

"Our ships sunk!" she exclaimed, then regained her composure "Vast portions of our navy have been destroyed…. What was it you asked?"

"Where's Pearl Harbor?"

"It is a major United States base in Hawaii. A naval base on the island of…" Her mother turned around. "I do not know the island. I shall go and ask your father."

In tense jerks Arthur pointed to the outside windowsill where noisy sparrows beat up white storms around a crust of bread. "They—war—about—my—toast."

"I'm going downstairs. Do you want me to turn on your radio?"

"Music—"

There was only news.

In the living room Phyllis's father sat at his desk, her mother behind him. "Oahu," he said. I'm not sure that's the right pronunciation, but we'll know soon enough. It's on every radio station."

The Sunday newspaper lay on the desk, rotogravure section on top. Phyllis stood beside her mother, looked down at the photograph of evergreens in a fairyland of snow.

"How unprepared we were!" her father exclaimed. "Phyllis…" Her father patted her arm too hard. "Merry Christmas, Phyllis. Our parents' generation gave us our war 'to end all wars,' now we're giving you yours. Your children…"

"John!"

"Excuse me, Deirdre. I forgot. Life will all be serenely beautiful for Phyllis—if we can only keep her from seeing it."

Phyllis went back upstairs, away from her mother's sugar coating and her father's barbs. Arthur, small and crumpled, was looking out of the window. "The—angry—birds—they— fly—in—the—sky—like—men—in—airplanes."

Phyllis's picture of Japan floated to her consciousness from "The Mikado": yellow men with water-flowing voices and ridiculous laws, smiles showing crescents of white teeth. Now the comedy had become a very different reality that expanded Phyllis's awareness of war from Europe to Asia. Planes, fighters, pilots. Suddenly Phyllis knew: *George will fight.*

She remembered a Sunday morning in the long-past summer when George had shown her one of his model airplanes, the one he had just finished. She marveled at his workmanship; such delicate painting, even the flag with forty-eight perfect stars. A pretty piece of art, and now...

"It's like seeing monsters out of a nightmare," Phyllis said.

"What—can—I—do?"

She shook her head. "I guess neither one of us..." With bullet speed, Phyllis's imagination killed George, then as quickly, her pain denied the thought. "I know he'll go. I'll miss him a lot."

"I—be—here."

"I know. But George will enlist. He'll be in danger." Arthur's head was down so that Phyllis could not see his face. "I feel like I really need to talk to him."

"I'm—here." Arthur's need tied Phyllis to Miss Bitzer's chair.

She heard her mother's step, and for once it was welcome. She stood at the top of the ramp, a wisp of her white hair flying out of order. "Miss Bitzer is ill today. It is nothing serious, I am sure." One by one she pulled the fingers of her left hand. "I must stay with Arthur this afternoon, so you and your father will go without me to *A Midsummer Night's Dream.*

"I'd forgotten."

"It has been a difficult morning. It will be good for you to get away." She left them in the silence.

Arthur's focused eyes, the one sure control he had, held Phyllis.

Another step in the hall. Phyllis sprang to her feet and started for the door just as George's muscled body came to fill it. They said "Hi" with the same breath.

"I wanted you to come."

He did not answer, just kept walking toward her, walking down the ramp, looking at Phyllis hard with a face she did not know, face set in anger. She backed away. He took her hand, reached for the other too, but it was behind her back. He squeezed her knuckles hard together. "Them dirty Japs!" His eyes and then his arms pulled her against him.

"Where can we go?" His urgency frightened Phyllis as much as it excited. He bent to kiss her.

She heard the sound of Arthur's hand striking the edge of the table. "Not here," she whispered.

"Him?" he said between the kisses that were buried in Phyllis's hair as she ducked her head. "It don't matter about..."

Phyllis pulled George toward the door erasing the rest of his sentence. She led him down the backstairs, down the long hall to the door at the end. "Let's go down in the basement. No one will be there." They walked quickly, quietly, she holding hard to his hand, afraid to let it go, as she led to the door at the head of the basement stairs. They heard its oiled click, hurried down clean steps that didn't creak. Then they were standing on the concrete floor with all the stone of the house solid above them.

Open rooms were not for holding closeness. They walked past the heat of the furnace room. Phyllis stopped, feeling the hot air creep up around her legs. The small door across from them was thick and heavy. "That's the wine cellar," Phyllis said.

"I know."

"There's no wine in it. Just my father's old camping stuff."

"I know."

The door was fitted with brass hardware, but the padlock spread open. George lifted the locking bar. They stepped inside, safe from the world in the small tight room smelling of canvas, old smoke, rough limestone—only a glimpse before George pulled the door shut. Darkness absolute. Air of their breath made their own small sky.

"I feel so..." Phyllis's voice trailed into a silence filled with turbulent sensation.

Hand hard around her arm. "I'll take care of you. I'll keep our country safe for you."

Heroism became a real and present thing, and she opened her heart to the strength of the love his words expressed. She felt her need of parents fading into childhood.

Phyllis drew back against the wall. Sand from the limestone flaked off under her hands; light sound of it sifting to the floor. "Sands of time," she whispered as she remembered her childhood fear of this dungeon place.

"What's the matter? Don't be afraid. I'm not getting into the fight for awhile." Groping through the dark, touching her, gently this time. "I'll keep you safe."

Holding to each other, life of their bodies pressing until Phyllis felt, even heard, the same blood flowing through them both.

"Here," he whispered. "There's a pile of soft stuff." Phyllis gave to his power as he pulled her down close beside him until they were half sitting and half lying on a pile of rough cloth. His hand covered her breast, its small shape fit his palm. His fingers moved faster, working at the buttons of her shirt, finally open, his hand slid underneath, then came tight under her bra, rough against her naked skin.

His hand left her breast. Out of the dark, it came down on her leg. Her body filled with excitement that exceeded sensation. She tried to stop her trembling as his hand slid up her thigh.

"Ooh—oh God, you're beautiful!" The breath of his words filled her with a core of unfamiliar emotion that left no room for thought. The heat of his fingers between her legs touched her love with a new language, and her moist response was first strange, then embarrassing.

Abruptly his hand left her, then the abrasive rasp of his zipper, told her what lay ahead and filled her with fear and guilt. She murmured a small frightened, "No," just as a sound stopped his action and drew all their attention. Light flooded through the door.

Open blouse, her skirt pushed up. A man. Her father!

George became a strange boy with sweat-damp hair stuck to his forehead; he pushed it back with a sooty hand. He said something, but it wasn't a word. He ducked past the rigid silhouette of Mr. Dean. He ran away.

Left alone. Phyllis closed her arms over her chest as terror stiffened her body. Her eyes shifted from her father's face before she had time to focus. He blocked escape. His voice struck her with judgement, "What's going on here? Did he hurt you?"

"Don't blame him." Her voice quivered as he walked toward her. "Leave me alone!" She exclaimed with the fear of a cornered animal. She started to run, but a hand met her chest, shoved her hard to the floor. The small pain was more surprise than hurt, even a welcome diversion from her mental pain.

"Are you all right? I didn't mean to push so hard." He reached to help her up. "I'm sorry." Phyllis stared at his open hand as he continued to speak. "I don't know what to say." His hand was strong and steady. "Phyllis, of course I'm angry. I'm disappointed by this behavior, but more than that. I'm frightened for you."

Phyllis felt his hand about to withdraw. Still clutching her blouse, she reached out letting him pull her up.

"That's better." He released her hand. "Now straighten yourself up."

She turned her back to button her blouse.

"I can't imagine what you see in that boy. You're a sensitive, intelligent person, and…"

"You…" The more she wanted to stamp and scream, the tighter she held it in. "You don't know him, and you don't know me."

"Phyllis, I'm not judging you! But *think!* What do you and that boy have in common? Yes, he's smart and quick to learn mechanical things, but that's not enough."

"I love him." Her words came out small as a child's and without the courage of conviction. She wished for George, strong beside her—even if his face was sweaty and smeared with basement soot.

"Darling, darling! Love can be quick to deceive. Sex may feel magical, but like everything else, it has to deal with the real world. Believe me, I know. It's a very physical thing with very physical consequences. You have an adult body, and you need to take adult responsibility. Are you ready to commit your life to George, to have his baby?"

"No!"

"Is that all you have to say to me?"

"But we didn't! We weren't going to." Phyllis hung her head down as she straightened her skirt, then continued to look at her feet. She crossed her arms over her chest, holding her love like a dead puppy.

From the house above them, Phyllis heard her name called, then repeated. "Mother's calling. I've got to go."

"I'm sorry. We still need to talk about this."

"Not now."

"One thing more. I wasn't spying on you. I just came down here to look for my navy uniform."

Phyllis ran up the basement steps two at a time.

"Where have you been?" A strand of her mother's hair had come unpinned and brushed her shoulder.

"In the basement."

"In the basement! At least nine of our ships have been completely sunk, and you not even aware! More news is coming all the time. But I did not mean to talk about this…. It is too cruel!" Phyllis felt her mother's hand on her shoulder, felt the hand saying, *Dear Child*. Then Mrs. Dean slipped under a cheerful mask: "Now then, *A Midsummer Night's Dream*. At times like these we all can use a diversion. But with Miss Bitzer sick again, my place is here. It is time for you to get ready for the matinee."

●

Her father's gloved hands on the steering wheel seemed to exist independently from the rest of him. His fingers flickered, and his hands rested only briefly in the same position. Phyllis was tense, expecting more talk about George.

"This is a strange time for fairyland," he said.

"Yes," she responded, both relieved and surprised.

She had seen magic in George's model airplanes and heroics in his strong and patient work as, without complaint, he helped his father, lifting, carrying, shoveling snow and stoking the furnace in the winter, gardening in the summer. Now all of it changed as she walked outside their intimacy and saw with a public view, like an ice palace, magic inside, but all wrong through outside eyes: black ice melting in the sun. Like the icy magic in the ice cave under the garage—"crud from Pa washing the car...Sort of a sewer-like." "I'll keep our country safe for you," George said, but then he ran away. As his strength melted away from her, she was left without the romantic cover for the small things that bothered her: the way he treated Arthur—his voice as he said "him"—as though Arthur was only a thing.

Her father's words penetrated Phyllis's consciousness in snatches. "...I didn't mention to your mother what happened this morning. To some degree, I understand." Phyllis's intense embarrassment blocked her ability to say *thank you*, and her father did not make the effort to continue. After a long emotion-filled silence, he changed the subject. "Our extra ticket won't be wasted. A friend of mine is joining us, my assistant, Marsha Jeffries."

Although her father spoke casually, Phyllis felt importance in the name. She had met Marsha in her father's store: the strong woman patiently helping a child choose a backyard tent or fitting a muscled climber with mountaineering boots and crampons. When Marsha spoke to people, her face seemed animated by a confident warmth propelled by her athletic body.

Their car stopped in front of a red brick building on the crest of the hill just before it dropped steeply toward downtown.

Phyllis could look through the bay windows of the downstairs apartment to a jungle of plants and flowers. The head behind the plants moved back, and Marsha was out of the door before her father had reached the apartment steps.

Although Marsha greeted her warmly, Phyllis was glad when Marsha, who was almost a stranger, caught on that Phyllis did not feel like talking and accepted her silence as she half-listened to their animated conversation. When they spoke of food and restaurants, Marsha's comment emerged, outrageously, from the flow of conversation. "I like strong cheese—cheese that smells like the feet of angels." Of course they spoke of the Japanese attack, but the bad news outside of her only plunged Phyllis more deeply into her personal troubles.

Phyllis's preoccupation with her own shattered dreams was too intense to be alleviated by the jumbled dreams of Shakespeare's midsummer night.

After the romantic confusions of the play, Phyllis came home to her own *"darkling night."* From her bed, she looked up at the ceiling of her room and remembered the open freedom of Marsha's conversation with its eager probing, warm interest, and the way her father laughed about "the feet of angels." *With Marsha, away from Mother, Father is a different person.*

Phyllis ran her hand over her breast and down her body—no response; her new body lost before it was found. She felt a sober aging as her father seemed suddenly younger. What she felt between her father and Marsha—but her mind seemed to blink like an owl in the sun, and Puck's words banished the incomplete thought.

> *"So quick bright things come to confusion…*
> *Be as thou wast wont to be;*
> *See as thou wast wont to see…"*

●

Phyllis did not see George until the following Saturday. He

came upstairs and stood in the hall outside her room while she was studying. "Phyllis, I gotta talk to you."

Without speaking she got up and followed him down stairs. She took his hand when they reached the front hall. From the strength of his grip, she felt a surge of the old intensity move up her arm and through her body. Six days ago she would have said, "I love you." Now, against her feelings, she led him into the library—the coldest room in the house.

They were standing in front of the wall of book cases and beside the statue of Venus. "I've enlisted," he said. "I go to boot camp a week from Monday." He pulled her to him, against her weak resistance, and looked earnestly into her eyes. "Will you wait for me?"

"I…" He stopped her words with a kiss.

Phyllis was too upset to respond as she would have just six days ago; but she didn't pull away from his urgent embrace, dreading what she intended to say when it was over. As she drew in her breath to tell him, he responded with another question. "Will you write to me?" She nodded her head.

Then he asked it, "Do you love me?" and Phyllis had to answer.

"It's not the same as it was," she said.

"I feel the same. I love you even more." His voice choked up so that it was hard for him to talk.

"I'll always like you," she said. "Only now everything is so different that…"

"But you don't love me?"

She answered slowly. "I guess not."

"Do I have a chance with you?"

How could she predict the future? Her mind groped through her emotions. "I'm sorry," was all she managed to say. "But all that happened—I'm not sorry about that."

"I'd marry you," he said.

Phyllis shook her head so that her hair flipped against her cheeks. "But I'm only sixteen—and college…" she broke off. It seemed unimportant. She could scarcely admit to herself that she was scared even to think of marriage.

"I'll write to you," he said.

Phyllis was relieved to see him go. She was afraid he might sob out loud, and it would be her fault. There would be only one way to comfort him, and now that had turned into a lie.

●

George was gone. Phyllis's aimless wandering led to Arthur's room. "I wanted to talk," she said.

"I—have—lots—of—time." Phyllis watched the beauty of his eyes transform his face.

Knowing how he disliked George, Phyllis couldn't tell Arthur about her last conversation with him and the cruelty and betrayal she felt guilty of. "I'm afraid of the war," she said. "Not of being bombed like London. More like it's a big dark cloud made out of hell or hate or evil. Something nobody really sees but everybody has to breathe. George enlisting. I knew it would happen, but I didn't know how it would be. Maybe he'll be killed and I'll never see him again, and that makes me feel just awful. I don't know. I don't really want him, but I don't want that black cloud to swallow him up."

In spite of his desire to see George gone, Arthur listened with sadness in his eyes.

"Another thing, I know so much more about my feelings about him than I ever knew about *him*—all the things we never said to each other. Just a few little unimportant things come out, dumb things to remember like he likes apple pie but not the Danish pastry his mother makes. The only important thing is he wants to be a pilot. He always has, and now that the war is here, he might get his dream. So I think he really likes the war. That scares me."

"Do—you—love—him?"

"Well, no, I guess I don't any more, but I miss the feeling a whole lot. Like I'm more in love with love than with George."

"Does—he—love—you?"

Phyllis nodded, thinking about marriage but not ready to talk about it. "I don't want loving to stop, like I'll lose something beautiful and never get it back, but... Oh, I don't know!" Phyllis stood, moved sharply to the window to shake away her confusion.

"Some—day—you'll—get—married."

"Not for a long time. I thought I'd always love George, but it was our private thing, and marriage seemed so far away. Now everything is so serious. Loving him always, that means marriage, and that makes it all different. When it was our private thing, George's grammar didn't seem important because love mattered so much more. But now I've been thinking about how a wedding would be—. I suppose George would go right on calling Father and Mother Mr. and Mrs. Dean. He acts like he's afraid of them. Then George would be your brother, and it bothered me the way he was with you. I just can't see him being your brother."

Phyllis saw agreement in Arthur's eyes. "I—don't—like—George."

Phyllis stayed in her private sadness until Arthur broke the silence.

I—won't—ever—get—married. Who—would—ever—want—me?"

Not true! Her shout was a silent wish; Arthur's knowing was rooted too deep to be pulled out with words that Phyllis reluctantly knew would be false.

Arthur in love? The look in his eyes, his smile somehow belonging to his own private world—yet the letter she wrote for him called to his mythical *Mary:* "I have a diamond."—followed by her guilty retreat to the bathroom without stopping to pick up his "diamond" rolling on the floor. That letter to his own imagination was as close as he had come to speaking with a girl his age. Phyllis tried to make a new picture. Is color behind the eyes of a blind man? sound in the inner ear of the deaf? physical desire trapped in Arthur's body?

First, to meet a person like himself, but he can't even hold her hand. Marriage? What could...

"May I share your company?"

"Oh, Mother."

Arthur addressed his mother in formal words without consonants. "How—are—you?"

"Fine, thank you, Arthur." Their mother sat down in Miss Bitzer's chair. "About what were you two so deep in thought? or am I intruding?"

Phyllis looked at Arthur waiting for him to speak.

In answer to her mother's questioning eye brows, Phyllis translated, *"Love."*

"What a welcome subject in these awful times! It is all-important to keep love in the family when the world shows so little of it."

Phyllis turned bold in the face of her mother's ignorance. "But Arthur doesn't mean that."

"Then?"

"He means a girl friend."

"What can our boy know of that?"

"Mother, he's nineteen years old. He feels... You tell her, Arthur."

His deep voice grabbed at the words. Phyllis took them one at a time as they were spoken. "I—want—to—meet—a—girl—friend."

Their mother stood, pain tightening her lips, concern lining her forehead. "My dear boy!" She walked behind him, smoothed his hair. "Some things are just not possible." She caught Phyllis's eye and pursed her lips in a warning for silence, then turned back to Arthur. "You will always have your family, and all of us love you very much."

"I—am—nineteen—years—old. I—want—to—be—a—man."

He looked for her response as Phyllis translated.

She took time to pull the fingers of each hand before saying, "It is very difficult to be a fully mature man. First he must go to college, then he must be able to get a job and go to work. He needs to talk to many people and write business letters. Oh, dear me! I know all this must be difficult for you to hear. I would so like to spare you. But there are so many dangers out in the world, and so many things to learn. Here your life can be safe, and you do not have impossible difficulties looming in front of you." With pain written across her forehead, she smoothed Arthur's hair back from the pain across his, then left the room, flicking her hand for her daughter to follow.

Not ready to leave Arthur, Phyllis put a hand on his arm.

His head turned from side to side so violently that his body swayed with it. He looked at her with his loneliness turned inside out. "I—saw—him—kiss—you." He continued, and Phyllis knew without hearing the words that he was asking what it felt like. She shook her head.

"I—want…" He didn't finish.

"I want too," Phyllis responded. "It's hard to know what we want until we find it. Sometimes we think we've found it, and then it isn't real—not what we really want."

"Like—George?"

"Yes, but it's different for you. I just don't see any way."

"If—I—could—get—out—in—the—world—meet—someone.

Phyllis shook her head. "I'd better go." Reluctantly she went toward her mother's room. There, under the light of a chandelier with crystals dropping down from a mirror plate, she saw her mother changed—thinning white hair, her face white too. The light drew hard lines: straight ones between her eye brows, straight ones down from her nostrils to the corners of her mouth, then down again below her mouth. Her head shook in denial. "You have no idea how difficult this conversation has been for me. More than anything I have tried to spare him the pain waiting for him in the outside world."

Phyllis blurted out, "But we can't do that! We should listen to him, try to give him some choices. There must be some place….Somewhere he could meet people."

Mrs. Dean shook her head. "He has you. You give him a great deal of young company in an appropriate way. He would be a very lonely boy without you."

Phyllis was not ready to accept her mother's compliment. "He's lonely anyway."

"There is no way to satisfy him; we must face his condition. You know I see to his care in the very best way I can, as perfectly as possible. We can keep him clean, neat, nutritiously fed. And we can do something else…. We can keep him innocent, protect him from the pains of facing a hostile world."

"Mother! He doesn't want that."

"Only because he doesn't know from what he is being spared."

Phyllis exploded. "He doesn't feel 'spared' He feels like he's in a cage!"

"We know better. You know the long story, so many doctors! At first your father went with me, to New York, to Philadelphia, even west to San Francisco. So many specialists, so many prominent medical institutions! They all said the same hopeless things." She sighed deeply, was about to continue.

"…that you should put him in an institution," Phyllis broke in, knowing her mother wouldn't say it.

"Finally, I went to Dr. Bates, your grandfather's doctor in Boston. Perhaps not as scientific as some of the specialists, but he was kind and understanding. He advised isolation for Arthur. That way I could protect him from the reality of his handicaps and from trying things beyond his abilities. You see, comparing himself to normal people would be just too painful. So we chose to build a life for him at home, to provide an attentive nurse to take care of his every need…at least basic needs," she added.

Phyllis's frustrated words poured out, filled with emotion from her own life. She lumped all her imposed restraints in a ball of blame against her mother and knew that Arthur did the same. "He has other needs! You need to listen to him. He *has* abilities, and he wants to try them. He wants a chance to see *people*."

As she finished, Phyllis was pricked with awareness of her own anonymity at school. Her impenetrable exterior was all that her classmates could see, and Phyllis had no idea of how to let them in. The quotation they would choose to go under her senior picture in the Crest School year book had already been set: *"Along the cool sequestered vale of life, she keeps the noiseless tenor of her way."*—Thomas Gray

"There, there." Her mother was coming toward her; Phyllis wanted to run for her life, but she stood still under the hand softly stroking her head. "Mother..." Her thoughts were patted away until they became wordless as a baby's.

She escaped into her room and closed the door.

V

Phyllis's freshman year was finished. In front of 344 Crest Avenue, the cab door slammed behind her. Street lights brought out the shine on spring leaves and jeweled the dew-wet lawns as the cone of sound vanished down the deserted street.

Phyllis stood between leaving and arriving, between winter and summer, between child and adult, and saw her house become a "mansion" through a stranger's eyes. The front door of fragile glass, supported in its framework of finely crafted grillwork, drew the eye to its rigid delicacy, while the symmetrical facade of pale stone framed attention and prevented the eye from wandering. Inside, Phyllis knew, was a place where intricate emotions moved invisibly like the intellects of chess players: long incubation, one small move.

Like a visitor, Phyllis approached slowly carrying her suitcase. The dim lights downstairs shone behind closed curtains giving the house a blind appearance. But upstairs in Arthur's room the curtains were not pulled, and the light glared out into the dark. Even as she became senile, Miss Bitzer never forgot to close in the room at night, but now she was gone. A white image passed quickly in front of the window then disappeared toward the door before Phyllis had time to see it clearly.

Phyllis felt her past in incremental sizes, separate people but the same, like a Russian puzzle toy of egg-shaped women, each one hidden under a larger shell, the small ones still complete within. With Miss Bitzer gone, life was changing around Arthur too.

Phyllis rang the bell.

Light flooded the vestibule as her father opened the inside door. Phyllis felt joy augmented with something missed in childhood, or something found too young for memory and lost too soon. It cracked Phyllis's shell of adult control. "Daddy!" and when the door opened, she dropped her suitcase and stood on tiptoes, her cheek pressed against his, "I..." before she said *love* the shell returned and Phyllis regained her emotional reserve.

"Why didn't you call me? I would have liked to meet your train."

"There was a cab waiting, so it seemed like a good time to save your gas," Phyllis said, walking into the hall as her father picked up her suitcase and closed the door.

"I walk to work, so we get along fine with our A ration."

"That's good." Phyllis looked past her father to the living room. "Where's Mother?"

"As a matter of fact, your mother's in the hospital."

"What!"

Her father put a reassuring hand on Phyllis's shoulder. "She's all right now. But we were worried for a time. She had a hysterectomy, and..."

"Good heavens! Why didn't you tell me?"

"We discussed it, but your mother didn't want to upset you. She thought it might interfere with your final exams. Naturally, we were concerned about a malignancy...."

"You were concerned, so why shouldn't I be? I have a right to know too!"

"Since you would be home so soon, we thought..."

"Was it malignant?"

"No. She was operated on the day before yesterday and is coming along well."

"Should I call her?"

"It's too late now, but tomorrow she'll want to see you."

"Any more upsets?"

"Well, actually, yes. Here, let me take your coat." He put it on the bench beside his own. "Let's not hang them up. A little untidiness is good for the soul."

Laughing, they went into the living room, and Phyllis collapsed on the couch. "Okay, I'm sitting down. Now give me the rest."

"There've been a lot of changes in the household."

"Oh?"

"You know Miss Bitzer went to the nursing home?"

Phyllis pictured her always-old face, lips sucked away into the cave of her mouth. "Yes. Mother wrote me, *Home for the Friendless!* I can't believe it!"

"Fortunately they are changing the name, emerging from the Dark Ages. But that's not the end of the news. Now Hilda's gone too."

"Hilda?" a kitchen fixture, her pink arm coming strong from the white of her uniform as she crumbed the table with the pad she held moving with a snap like the end of a whip.

"She took a defense job. We can't blame her. High pay, highly patriotic. 'Rosy the Riveter' you know."

"Isn't she too old?"

"She was just your age when she came to work here, only eighteen, so she isn't as old as she seems to you," he answered with a smile.

"Remember? My birthday's in March. I'm nineteen."

"All right. I'll give you another year—but reluctantly. I'm in no hurry to have you out of here."

"But you were talking about Hilda."

"She had twelve younger brothers and sisters, so the work here was a lot easier on her than all she had to do at home, once she learned the ropes—your mother's ropes."

"Then who's left?"

"Carl, of course. The employment agency dug up some less-than-adequate day help, but Ilie fills in. Now that George is over seas, she's glad to have the job. You know her baking! I'm rounding out nicely on Danish pastry. With honey replacing short sugar rations, it's even stickier."

"Can they manage? With Arthur and everything?"

"Now for the final change. Arthur has a new nurse."

"What!"

"After you see her, you'll really exclaim! As a sequel to Miss Bitzer, she's incredible, a vivacious little beauty about your age."

"That's hard to believe! How does Mother take it?"

"I grabbed the first and only applicant. She's just out of nursing school. It was Mary or residential care for Arthur, something your mother agonized over. We nearly had to go that route. We'd even selected one, and I planned to take Arthur there the morning after I'd left your mother in Miller Hospital. Then, the evening I took your mother to the hospital, I got home to a ringing phone. It was Mary. After talking with her, I was almost sure she was the one for Arthur. She told me she didn't want hospital work and said she was willing to do whatever needed to be done."

"That's lucky," Phyllis commented. "In a house this size there sure is plenty to be done!"

Her father raised his eyebrows and nodded vigorously. "With the war absorbing so much labor, people are wonderful about taking up the slack. Of course we pay her a nurse's wages— plus a little. So without much trouble I managed to persuade her to come to us."

"I can't wait to meet her."

"Soon I'm sure. To continue the saga—early the next morning I canceled the application to The Home for Social Development, and the next day I hired Mary. She moved in that evening. Believe me! It was breathless activity."

"Then Mother hasn't even met her! Why the big rush? You could have asked me. I'm not useless you know—even if I can't cook," she added reluctantly. When she thought of her summer plans, a painting class at the gallery and time for swimming and reading, Phyllis was glad to escape major responsibility. Still, Arthur would have taken precedence in her life.

"Your mother and I decided long ago never to ask you to take over Arthur's care."

"Oh, Father! You know I'm willing." Yet she desperately needed the time to pursue her own life. For nearly as long as she could remember Arthur had absorbed a major part of her time and her emotions.

"We wouldn't ask it of you."

With war news continually exploding from the radio, the news reels and the papers, stay-at-homes were kept in a constant state of guilt. Phyllis's life, vacillating between a comfortable home and college seemed horribly self-indulgent. *No one ever asks me to do anything.* Yet she was afraid of how she would handle it if they did.

The room looked smaller than Phyllis remembered it, but the chemical smell of furniture polish was unchanged. "How deadly quiet this place can be!"

"It's a tight house." He looked toward the dark window.

"It's cold for June," Phyllis said.

He made no move toward the fireplace, yet Phyllis had the sensation that she was hearing his thoughts before he spoke. "I'll light the fire. It will feel good to be over-heated."

Flames licking the birch bark to black made moving patterns, seen and then forgotten.

"I thought I'd take a painting class at the gallery this summer."

"Sounds nice."

Desultory words became a distant background to their separate thoughts. Phyllis, recovering from late nights preparing for exams, started to yawn and was ready for bed early in the evening.

●

Mary was closing the door to Arthur's bedroom. "Night night, don't let the bed bugs bite. You bite 'em first!" She closed the door and was gone.

Arthur's brief laughter melted into dreamy quiet. The glow

from a distant street light spilled over his blue blanket turning it purple.

He closed his eyes and let his mind carry him close to Mary. The faint glow of the street light through his lids transformed to lights in Mary's hair. Her face was greater beauty than he ever imagined. He felt her quick hands as she washed him, the soapy cloth sliding over his body, then the rough towel rubbing him dry. He thought of the images in the art book Phyllis had given him when he was only sixteen, the nude in *Anyone Can Draw* that he had tried to paint and made such a mess of—. No one could paint Mary. *I wish Mary was nude beside me, and I could touch her skin.* But the dream was firefly quick. *She doesn't like me.*

His hand was trapped under his body, and it was too difficult to pull it free. His twisted body constricted his lungs, and he hurt as deeply as he could feel. *Someone to love me—all the time—*

Slowly the amorphous cloud that had been growing since his mother went away moved into him and covered his mind with fear. First Phyllis, then his mother, and some day Mary. All would go.

His hand stayed pinned under his body for a long time before it convulsed to freedom, and Arthur could sleep.

●

Phyllis and her father ate breakfast in the convenient comfort of the maids' dining room. Across the table where white rings marred the blue paint, her father scanned the paper for the details of battle news he had heard on the radio the night before. On her side of the paper, Phyllis saw the incongruous juxtaposition of palm trees evocative of luxurious resorts and the austere gray of battle ships.

She spread jam on her toast. He put down the paper, spooned honey on his Red River. "What are your plans for the morning?" he asked, pouring milk on his cereal.

"I want to see Arthur first, then mother, so I'll have something to talk to her about in the hospital."

"Yes...Oh, here's Mary!" Quick steps sounded on the stairs. Mary had that casual blond beauty one expects in a model advertising ski clothes, and her strong walk and easy "Hi" fit the same picture. The arc of her honey-toned hair swung easily against the white collar of her seersucker nurse's uniform. Phyllis wondered what her mother's reaction to Mary would be, then answered her own question with her mother's platitudes: *peaches-and-cream complexion; clear-blue eyes; wholesome girl...* Next her mother would say, "such a shame she uses too much lipstick." Yet it brightened Mary's face and animated the smile that played so freely with her features.

"Can you believe what I found in Arthur's room, right on his bed?" Mary held out her hand to display a striped caterpillar, black, white and yellow, "This worm!"

"A monarch larva. How strange, that it could have crawled so high!" Phyllis exclaimed.

"There was a strong wind last night," her father said, "but it's hardly probable that the wind could rip off a milk-weed leaf and blow it up against the window. The screen is loose at the bottom so however it got up there, it could have crawled in. I've been meaning to ask Carl to fix that screen."

"I didn't see any leaf," Mary said, "but it could've gotten through the screen all right. What should I do with it?" Phyllis found a mason jar and used an ice pick to punch holes in the cover.

Mary poured oil in a frying pan. "Arthur wants eggs this morning—I think. I asked him a bunch of yes-or-no questions, but I still have to guess what he's trying to say. He waggles his head all the time, so everything seems to be *no*." Mary spoke in an easy burst, at the same time asking to be liked and sure she would be. "How should I fix his eggs? Does he like fried or scrambled?"

Phyllis shook her head. "One never knows from one day to

the next." When she glanced at her father, she found his face as blank as hers. "Just fix them any way you like. I don't think he's too particular."

"I'll go upstairs with you," Phyllis said when the country-style eggs were ready. "They look good. Half fried, half scrambled. So they should suit him either way."

Phyllis took the caterpillar, ensconced in its jar, with her. Arthur would like to see the metamorphoses. She put it beside his breakfast tray on the table next to his chair.

"Hi." Phyllis leaned over the arm, bent down to kiss Arthur in the fenced way a wheelchair demands. "It's so good to see you! I brought you a hungry friend, but he prefers milkweed to eggs." Arthur slowly shook his head. "He'll be fun to watch." But Arthur gave no response.

"I'll give him his breakfast," she said to Mary.

"Okay, I'll leave you two to talk." Above her smile, Mary raised her eyelids acknowledging how difficult conversation with Arthur was.

In the oak outside the window two gray squirrels chased each other in a circle, and a flock of sparrows fluttered among the vines on the side of the house. Phyllis offered Arthur a spoonful of egg, but he refused.

"What do you want then?" she asked, disappointed that he showed no happiness in seeing her. The brightness had disappeared from his eyes making him look empty and spiritless. "What's the matter?"

Arthur's look was pleading.

"We can talk for a long time. I have the whole morning."

Phyllis felt his fear before he spoke. "Grandmother—is—gone."

"Yes. Everyone dies sometime. You're still thinking about that...?"

"Ahh—"

"Grandmother was old. For her it was time."

Phyllis had been away from his speech too long; now the clotted flow of importunate syllables forced her to make him repeat many words. "In—my—mind—I—kind—of—think—that—my—parents—are—going—to—die—too." One by one Phyllis repeated the words as he spoke them, meaning nearly lost in their separation.

"But not for a long time," she responded, finally.

In the shake of his head, Phyllis saw her simple answer discounted. "Every—body—needs—some—body."

"I know, but Mother's operation went fine. She'll take care of you, make sure you always have somebody."

"Some—day—she—won't. Then—the—whole—world—will—be—on—my—shoulders."

"I'll take care of you," Phyllis said when she finally understood the word *shoulders*. But her tone reflected her doubt.

"You'll—get—married."

She put her hand on his shoulder, ran it down his arm feeling his knotted biceps like a hard-rubber ball.

"Sometimes—I—wish—that—I—was—not—born—to—my—mother—and—my—father."

"But they love you." The time between his words magnified the inadequacy of her answers.

"I—hate—to—use—this—word—but—I—have—to."

When Phyllis looked at his face, she knew it: *cripple.*

"I—feel—like—I'm—in—prison. These—walls—would—disappear—if—I—could—walk."

Phyllis remained silent.

"I—just—have—to—stay—here—and—I—don't—know—what—to—do—with—my—life. I—hurt—inside. My—body—and—my—mind—hurt."

Phyllis pushed her fist into her hand. "But Arthur…" No use telling him not to worry; just listen.

"Every—two—days—my—thoughts—build—up—into—a—notion—that—I—don't—know—when—I'll—be—seeing—Mother—or—Father—die."

"But they're still young and healthy."

"George—" he said.

Phyllis was not sure whether Arthur was waiting for her to

respond or just tired. "Young people in the war, that's different. He could be shot down, but he probably won't be."

"Death—is—something—that—no—one—can—stop—not—even—Jesus. Grandma—too."

"Grandmother wasn't having fun any more; she was too sick."

"Where—does—your—mind—go—when—somebody—takes—you? Like—God?"

"What do you think?"

After a long struggle, Phyllis deciphered Arthur's answer. "Purgatory?" She could hardly believe the affirmation in his eyes. "Whoever told you that?"

"Miss—Bitzer."

"What!"

"It's—like—hell. It—burns—you—until—you—get—ready—for—heaven."

"There's no such place!" came Mary's sudden exclamation. "For you? Not so!"

When Phyllis turned to the voice, Mary was standing behind them with a glass of orange juice. "You surprised us. Arthur was asking about purgatory."

Mary glanced at Arthur's cold toast and congealed eggs, then smiled hopefully. "Now it's time for your juice. You must be thirsty after talking for two hours."

"You mean it's eleven thirty? I've got to get to the hospital! Mother must be wondering what happened to me," Phyllis said. "See you later."

Mary picked up the tray of cold food. "It's time you eat something," she said.

As Phyllis and Mary left his room, Arthur was still talking. "I'll be back in a few minutes," Mary called over her shoulder. "He's such a hassle to understand! By the time he gets to the end of a sentence, I've forgotten the beginning."

Phyllis grabbed a muffin from the bread box as Mary washed Arthur's dishes. "I really go for that shy smile of his," Mary said with an exuberant splash of soap suds.

"Me too," Phyllis agreed, then hurriedly slammed the backdoor.

●

Phyllis entered the sterile world of the hospital and checked the room number, 313, on the slip of paper her father had given her. She, the only occupant in the laboring elevator, felt as empty as it was—as though she were waiting for an adult self she had yet to meet. Her mother, helpless in a hospital bed, had left a vacant role Phyllis was not ready to fill.

Nurses and orderlies moved up and down the halls in gum-soled shoes. A rubber pad looped to the door knobs prevented the door from latching. Phyllis entered silently. She took a long look at the head resting on the pillow, eyes closed, hair fanned out and disappearing, ghostlike, into the white of the pillowcase. Without the customary powder and a touch of rouge and void of social expression, her face appeared naked. On the other side of the bed, a bud vase held two roses, one red, one white, looking so much more alive than the face next to them. As Phyllis considered whether to leave, then reenter with a knock, her mother's hand fluttered slightly under the sheet. "Mother?"

She opened her eyes, and the deathlike mask left her face.

"I'm so glad to see you. I'd almost given you up." Her voice was as thin as a child's.

"I stayed with Arthur for a long time. We talked."

"How is Arthur?"

Purgatory—but Phyllis's response contradicted her thought. "Fine. How are you?" As Phyllis bent over her small mother and kissed her, it seemed that their positions were reversed.

"I'm coming along fine." Under the surface of her mother's smile, Phyllis imagined a small girl grinning up bravely after skinning her knee.

Phyllis chose her father's words. "You're a good sport." Then she quickly spoke of Arthur. "He's coming along well." She left no time for questions, "Mary is cheerful and energetic, and she really likes Arthur."

Mrs. Dean's eyelids flickered. "Leaving him so suddenly like that, looking so alone and helpless…. I have been so worried."

Phyllis pulled the straight chair close to the bed and sat down.

"Who gave you the beautiful roses?"

Her mother's smile transformed the deep lines around her mouth to a delicate fan. "Your father." She gestured to the table. "Read the card."

In her father's straight-up writing she read: *"My Deirdre, here is a rose for each of our children. With love, John."*

"That's nice." Her mother nodded without the familiar crispness. "Which is which?"

"I think you are the red one, full of brightness and color. Arthur is white, pure and innocent."

Not always so pure and innocent, then Phyllis diverted her thought. "I was so surprised to find Hilda gone!"

"Yes, it was a shock to all of us—after all those years. A mere child when she came to us. I grew very fond of her," then she added sadly, "I don't think she knew it, not until the day she left. We gave her a gold chain with a ruby pendent when she left us. I'm sure she knew she was appreciated. I saw tears in her eyes."

"What a nice thing to do!" Surprise rang in Phyllis's exclamation. "I wouldn't have guessed any of that. I never really knew her. I only saw what she did, and she never became a real person to me."

"I don't think she liked children very much. She had too many of them at home. With us she was always attentive to duty. I don't know how we will ever replace her. Adequate domestic help is almost impossible to find. All the girls are getting defense jobs. But of course we should not expect life to be easy in these trying times, my problems… I am being too too selfish."

The old record back; Phyllis was surprised to feel herself welcoming the familiar, even her own impatience at her mother's martyr role.

"It will all work out," Phyllis said.

Her mother's gaze drifted. "I remember how it used to be, during the depression—after Edie left—I had thirty-one applicants for a nursemaid position. I tried one after another. None of them were able to get along with you children. But Edie..." The softness in her tone was gone with the next sentence. "She was a mistake. Such strange ways, so indulgent with you children and somehow enveloping, and that dark look... Almost frightening. I think of the pied piper leading, one cannot know where."

Phyllis was glad to see a nurse come with water, a glass straw and a little white envelope. Another followed with equipment for taking blood pressure. "It looks like time for me to leave." Phyllis kissed her mother, lips brushing her white hair. "Take care of yourself." She turned in the doorway. "Arthur misses you."

"Tell him I miss him too." Her voice sounded stronger, and she raised her head from the pillow.

It was a beautiful day, and Phyllis walked the ten blocks home, glad not to be closed into the yellow box of a streetcar. Shiny-clean leaves, birds and flowers were bursting with their annual defiance of winter's death.

Before entering the house, she went down the garden steps and all the way to the back gate where weeds had been allowed to grow. She picked milkweed for Arthur's caterpillar and took it to his room, hoping she was not too late to intercept starvation for the trapped worm.

Arthur was listening to *Superman* on the radio when Phyllis left him.

●

Superman had flown over the clouds, and a powerful voice was extolling "Wheaties, breakfast of champions." Arthur banged at the rod his father had affixed to the power switch of his radio—over and over until he succeeded in shutting off the offending voice.

Mary makes the whole world into a good place. Some day Mary will go away. Then the sun will go out. Arthur knew; these halcyon days would end. He looked into the solid permanence of his oak tree where sparrows tossed through the green like dead leaves blown by a twisty wind. *Does the wind make their feathers feel like Mary brushing my hair?*

Until now Arthur's restricted experience had dealt him a short hand, and his life was an endless reshuffle of the few cards permitted in his niggardly deck. Now his slowly emerging instincts pushed him to reach for the missing ones he was never told existed.

Mary came into his room with Phyllis.

"It's only been a week. I still need help understanding you, Arthur."

"I—teach—you." That was funny, but they couldn't laugh until Phyllis translated.

"And I thought Latin was hard!" Mary exclaimed.

"What—is—Latin?"

She understood!

"It's a language I had to learn so I could know the names of bones and medicines: all that kind of stuff. Easy words like tibia and ulna, and hard ones like cerebrovasclar and hydroxychloroquine. But you don't have to know that stuff."

"I—want—to—know—what—you—know."

Mary exchanged glances with Phyllis, then asked Arthur, "Why don't you tell me what you know instead?"

"I—can—write—a—story—for—you."

"Phyllis has to help me some more first."

Phyllis and Mary went away, talking to each other.

Arthur's unspoken wish followed them, *I want to talk more.*

●

As they left Arthur, Mary led the way with long easy strides toward the back stairs. Phyllis, her steps lagging, looked after the tall girl crowned with shining blond hair: *Anybody would like Mary.* Arthur's voice pursued them down the hall, and Phyllis felt her place in his life inexorably slipping toward Mary. A cloud of envy shaded her affection for the experienced nurse, and she longed for equal skills. They halted at the door to the back stairs.

"I'm going to make custard for Arthur's desert," Mary said, her capable hand on the doorknob.

"I can't cook anything." Phyllis giggled, hating herself, first for her incompetence, then for admitting it. As Arthur's voice again reached out to them, a sudden memory of her first understanding of Arthur's words came to her rescue: *Open the door.* She felt the wings of that first thrill beating in her chest as her restless fingers raked her tight curls from her neck and pushed them up over her ears. Yes, she did know more about Arthur than anyone else did. But the sad crash of that fated bird so long ago didn't fit this casual time. Phyllis stared at a small freckle on the back of Mary's hand as it turned the doorknob.

When the door opened, Phyllis blurted out, "Arthur has an obsession with birds, and he writes about them ad nauscam." Phyllis gave a self-conscious giggle as she realized how lightly her words discounted Arthur's perceptions and betrayed the depth of her understanding.

Mary turned in the doorway, the sun streaming from the window over the stairs behind her, back lighting her with the glow of a Renaissance angel. "That's how it is with people who want to get free," Mary said. "Like old women with their canaries. My grandma, she used to buy as much bread for the birds as she did for herself. Her arthritis was real bad, and she loved to watch the pigeons and sparrows fly when she was lying on her bed. As a kid, I used to put crumbs out on the windowsill for her birds."

As Mary started down stairs, Phyllis said, "I know. Arthur likes that too, looking for a life outside himself, like your grandmother."

Phyllis went to her room, her conflicted emotions sinking

her into depression. Her first assignment for her art class at the gallery was due on Monday. It did nothing to cheer her up. She had expected the class to be fun; but, unable to find a painter willing to teach the class, the gallery substituted an art therapist who looked into her students with prying eyes and asked intrusive questions, as the assignment demonstrated: "Self-portrait of yourself as an animal." Phyllis was too incensed with the teacher to work on the assignment until she switched her focus from herself to Arthur.

She filled two pages of her sketch book with multi-colored birds, the two final ones attacking each other like fighting cocks. She delighted in their rage.

When absorption in her work took her beyond irritation with the task, Phyllis painted a tiger with stripes as brilliant as Mary's hair, its form camouflaged behind stripes of sun and shade.

Like a gripping story, her images compelled her. Dinner interrupted her work, and she gulped it down, then hurried back to her room. The tiger needed a cage; she rushed to the basement in her search for wire to make one. On Carl's work bench, she found a spool of copper wire in a wooden soap box. *"Yes!"* she exclaimed aloud. The box could be the house—her house. She painted it stone gray and drew in the windows on either side of the front door in ridged balance, then the door itself, but the iron vines holding the glass ended up looking like prison bars, and the house looked small and weak. Phyllis sawed away one side of the box and concentrated on the interior.

Back in her room, she cut out the tiger then fenced it with the wire. From black pipe cleaners she twisted a large spider which she suspended from the box cover. Its legs held, as though they were part of its web, the wire bars that caged the tiger.

To change the fighting cocks to one bird without an adversary, she cut out the two and glued them together with cotton stuffed between them. She wrapped the paper bird with white silk thread, as though it were a captured fly, until only one wing was visible. Phyllis glued the tightly webbed bird into a corner of the house, a strand of the web still attached to the spider's spinnerets.

Although she had worked quickly, Phyllis's craftsmanship satisfied her in its details, and she could look beyond her technique to the images which seemed to have passed through her. She was looking into a stage set that had constructed itself, and the play it was staging questioned: *What if all this energy breaks free...?*

Phyllis had no idea of the time until she heard her father's tread on the steps. So it must be after eleven. Impulsively she ran into the hall. "I've finished my art assignment," she said.

"Oh?" He seemed preoccupied.

"Do you want to see it?" she asked eagerly.

"It's late," he said. "But I can take a look."

It's the whole story of our life. Would he understand?

He stood over her looking down at the display on her desk. "Well, that's quite a hodgepodge," he said.

To me it's all so clear! The excitement of creation drained away. Her voice flattened. "You don't understand, do you?"

"Explain it to me." It was hard to tell from the tone of his voice if he really wanted to know or if he was just tired.

She needed to make some emotional connection to her father but felt none. To explain, she would have to stop the speed of creativity and move slowly into reverse. "I can't think how," she said. "It's just not a word thing."

"Phyllis, I'd really like to know." He leaned over her desk and studied the model, then groped for something to say. "Is it some kind of a fantastic zoo?"

She shook her head.

"Can you tell me what the assignment was?" he asked hopefully.

"We were supposed to depict ourselves as animals," she said reluctantly.

He looked again. "It's coming clear, our house." He studied it silently for a long time. "Yes, now I see."

When she looked up at him, she knew he did. She reached up as he bent down to kiss her and hugged him tightly.

"You've said a lot," he said. It was enough. She went to bed content.

●

Mary had left his bedroom with his toothbrush and his washing bowl. Arthur was lying in his bed staring at the door, waiting for Mary.

She came back, and she took his hand when she said good night. He waited for her to say her joke about the bed bugs. She said it and closed the door.

Mary likes me. If I were a man standing up, I would kiss her good night.

Arthur stayed awake for a long time, dreaming, but not asleep. He could run on a branch like a squirrel. Then he felt like Superman flying without wings.

In the morning he tried: *I'm a bird, I'm a plane, I'm Superman.* It was wrong; he was a cuckoo bird. *Mary can't like me.* That day he told her a story to write.

"One day last week I see a purple bird, and he was going crazy because he was a cuckoo bird in love. He sat in my head and did thoughtless singing. He flew around the room, but he always landed on my head. He was cuckoo! He had a long nose, and he had a long tail. Everywhere he went, he sang: 'Cuckoo, cuckoo, cuckoo' until he flew out the window and took a nose dive right on his beak. Then he did something no bird ever did before. He took off to find the wild blue yonder. He flew all over the world, but he couldn't find any wild blue, and he searched all over, but he still couldn't find any blue yonder. He even searched the ground and the heaven.

"Then he was too down to know what it's like to be a bird, so he fell on his nose into the dark ground."

"Read—out—loud."

"Okay. I'll get Phyllis. She'd like to hear this one."

As Phyllis heard Arthur's words, for the first time, in a voice other than her own, she was hit with the conflict between his expanding world and her bond to his old one, like a mother sending her child off for his first day at school.

Mary's laughter ran over the surface of Arthur's story and interrupted her reading, but Phyllis looked for the yearnings underlying his words. She saw his struggle to communicate to Mary, then, to gain Mary's acceptance, covering his feelings with a camouflage of jokes. Could Mary hear the heartbeat of his story?

Perhaps Mary saw Phyllis's unasked question. "When a laugh runs by, I gotta catch it quick." She sobered quickly. "...the war and all." Mary gave her attention to Arthur. "You don't want that beautiful bird to end up in the ground!" Phyllis saw his neglected spirit beneath the mask of his clown-bird, but Mary addressed the action, "I want to know what happens next."

Arthur responded, "He—came—out."

"Bravo!" Mary exclaimed. "Cuckoo came out of the ground! He just won't stay down, will he?"

Arthur tipped his head back and opened his mouth to the roses on the valance of the curtain. *I wrote a good story.* But Phyllis heard the laughter as superficial.

Arthur looked at Mary's face, looked out at a happy world. "It's such a beautiful day, and your caterpillar needs new leaves. Let's Phyllis and me bring you outside with us," Mary said. She had talked to Phyllis about taking Arthur out, but Phyllis would not have chosen to spring the idea so abruptly. The icy experience with George had been too frightening.

Yet Arthur quickly approved.

As Phyllis disentangled Arthur's fingers from the wheel-spokes of his chair, Mary took the caterpillar in its jar of droppings and wilted leaves. Together, Mary behind and Phyllis in front, they rolled Arthur's chair out the kitchen door and down the steep rough stones of the garden steps.

Phyllis picked milkweed for the caterpillar, then put the jar under Arthur's chair to shade its occupant, contentedly munching a design of scallops in a fresh leaf.

Mary picked a bouquet of iris, then started for the garden steps. "Now I'm going to make that beef stew for tonight," she said, so casually. Phyllis was acutely aware of her ignorance in the kitchen.

In spite of a fly on his nose, Arthur remained focused on the spot where Mary had disappeared. Phyllis brushed away the fly.

He opened his mouth and waited for the taut cords in his throat to loosen. Now—I—am—learning—what—the—world—is—like. How—to—look—out—at—it. I—do—not—want—Mary—to—go—EVER. I—am—pretty—near—a—man—now—and—I—think—it—is—time—to—grow—up."

Phyllis repeated his words as they came, but answered them with silence.

"Did—you—ever—get—drunk?"

"No. Why do you ask?"

"People—do—it. I—want—to. It—turns—my—world—cuckoo."

"I guess it does. Once in college I went out with a boy who got drunk. His name was Larry Dingle. He walked sort of like a bear because one leg was shorter than the other. That's why he was 4-F. He joked all the time, so I never knew his serious side."

"You—mean—he's—cuckoo?"

"Like your story? I guess everybody has their own kind of cuckoo. Larry was smart in science, and everybody thought he was fun. But he wasn't sensitive like you."

"Like—George?"

"Larry was different. I never really liked him. I didn't even know him before he asked me for a date. He said, 'I like your wild hair.' I hate it." Phyllis raked it up with her fingers making it more unruly than ever.

"Why—did—you—go?"

"I guess I just wanted a date." Arthur was waiting for more. "I guess I wanted love. It was a dumb place to look for it. I remember the night. It was raining, and the city lights glittered in the oily gutters. It was like seeing stars where there weren't any. Then the place he took me to, it was a strip joint. Larry told me, 'It'll do you good to see the world.' Maybe that's why I followed him, not wanting to behave like a naive child."

"What—is—a—strip—joint?"

"Women take off their clothes, and men watch."

"Why?"

"I don't know. I hated it. People were getting drunk, and it was disgusting. I went into the rest room. I cried, and then I got a cab and went back to the dorm."

Arthur wanted to know more, but Phyllis only half explained. "It's sex. Men want something they can touch, or at least look at."

"I—want—to—touch—love. I—would—touch—her—gentle." Arthur's hand was clenched into a fist. He was watching a bee struggle into a snapdragon. "How—did—I—come—to—be?" Arthur was a man of twenty two.

"Mother and Father had sexual intercourse, but I can't imagine that they did it without any clothes on. I imagine the room was dark, they were under the covers, and Mother's night gown was up just far enough. I imagine she didn't like it very much. She was thinking about violets in her new hat or whether they'd have roast lamb for dinner." By the time she had finished, he had forgotten to ask what sexual intercourse was.

After a thoughtful pause, Arthur signaled to a bag Mary had hung from the back of his chair. It held his writings. Phyllis regarded Arthur's stories as her personal buried treasure, and now that Mary had joined the search, Phyllis sometimes felt excluded. She read eagerly:

"I was going in a car, but I didn't know where because it's hard for me to put two and two together..."

"But, Arthur, you know..." Arthur closed both his eyes in a wink. Phyllis smiled. "Okay, I get it."

"On the road, I asked my chauffeur to stop the car and let me

out. He did, and I looked under the car. There was a girl's face looking back at me. I thought I knew her, but not for sure. It might be Mary, or it might be my imagination. I asked my chauffeur if he saw it, and he didn't. It made me consider. It's very simple. She's here, but she isn't here. It's a vision...."

"But, Arthur, I don't understand why she's under the car." He merely gave her a knowing look.

We went to the courthouse and got a marriage license. We went to a church, and I saw Mary there. We talked about getting married, because there's one thing that stops me. If Mary can walk, she would walk way out of my life. We decided not to get married."

Phyllis had difficulty understanding the last choked sentence. "I like it. But the end is so sad."

"I—don't—know—how—mother—would—take—it."

"That doesn't matter when it's just a story." Phyllis stood up, knowing that it was more than a story.

She saw his random twitching that told her *don't go*, but she had to get to the hospital. "It's late, and I've got to visit Mother. I'll read her your story."

Phyllis found Mary, and together they struggled up the garden steps pulling and pushing Arthur in his chair. He was talking, but it was impossible to understand him above the commotion as the chair clanked over the stones.

Phyllis left Arthur's room to the sound of his voice talking to Mary.

●

As she walked to the hospital, Phyllis contrasted the complexity of the world she moved through with Arthur's dream world as it emerged from his immobile life in abbreviated word skeletons and without an intellectual critique.

Although Phyllis knew Arthur's story would upset and confuse her mother, she had an urge to break into Mrs. Dean's complacent denial.

Phyllis found her mother sitting in an arm chair. It was late, and she stayed only long enough to read Arthur's story aloud. Her mother listened intently, her face reflecting conflicting love and pain. "I would never have guessed that he would have such thoughts! That he would tell them to you!"

"I didn't know whether to tell you...."

"I am glad you did. I should know." There was so much sadness in her voice. "I thought we had protected him so well."

"I'm sorry." Phyllis kissed her mother good bye.

●

In the evening Phyllis and her father were sitting in the living room, he behind his paper.

"Arthur is in love with Mary."

The paper came down with a vigorous rustle.

"...in his own way."

"Did Mary tell you that?"

"No, Arthur, in his own way. A story."

"Don't be silly, of course he loves you." She returned his smile. "I don't know what that boy would have done without you."

Phyllis shook off her father's compliment; Arthur wanted more than a sister's love.

"He must be angry," her father said. "Really angry with the endless restraints on his life."

"But he seems so gentle," Phyllis said. "—most of the time," she added, thinking of George.

"Maybe that's because his anger is like a boomerang. It never reaches out to touch another, only comes back to hit him."

"I wouldn't have thought of it that way."

Again he smiled that crooked smile. "You never threw a boomerang." He was quickly serious. "It's so for all of us, to some degree; our own anger always circling back at us."

Phyllis got up slowly, went into the hall to get Arthur's story from her purse. As her father read, she watched sadness and amusement take turns across his face. "Arthur is a complicated young man," he mused, "but without action and a narrow vocabulary narrowing his thought.... It's hard to believe he is twenty-two years old."

"Today he asked me how he came to be."

"That's a tough one."

Her father went back behind his paper. He held it for a long time without turning a page, then lowered it. "It's fortunate Arthur didn't ask your mother to field that one."

Phyllis giggled self-consciously.

"I've got a story to tell on your mother now that you're old enough to be amused." He uncrossed his long legs and leaned toward Phyllis. "Deirdre had gotten a novel for your grandfather for Christmas, one she hadn't read. Before she wrapped it, she decided to read it. Well, it seemed there was a page that wasn't pure enough for your grandfather's gentle sensibilities, so your mother did the obvious thing. Very carefully, with a razor blade, she sliced out the offending page."

"What!" Phyllis was laughing so hard she missed the next sentence.

"That should have been the end of it, but your mother didn't reckon with your grandfather's resourcefulness. A couple of weeks after Christmas she got a letter from him saying that the book was missing a page, so he wrote the publisher, and they sent him a new copy."

Reluctantly they let the laughter run down. Again her father shielded his face behind the news. Phyllis was about to go to her room when the rustle of paper stopped her. She could not tell whether he was angry or sad.

"From the beginning your mother couldn't let Arthur come into the world. Her body, like the clamp of a vise, holding him even then...for forty eight hours. She has never known that some things have to take their natural course. Fear, fear of everything beyond the control of her will..." He folded his paper.

Phyllis left the room slowly, confused by her father's words.

Although she planned to go to her own room, Phyllis passed by, then turned back and opened her mother's door instead. The room had been cleaned, then left too quickly. The bedside table was still pulled out from the wall. Phyllis was about to push it back when she was attracted to a slender volume of Emily Dickinson's poems on top of it. Not surprisingly, the spine sprang open to her mother's favorite poem. Tucked between the pages was an old photograph, and Phyllis realized she was staring down into her mother's childhood. The elaborate costume prompted Phyllis to think of her mother preserved in a Victorian sachet and squeezed between the pages of two world wars, as innocent of the change her generation wrote as a pressed rose.

"After great pain, a formal feeling comes—" Phyllis read it through, all the way to *"letting go—"*. She felt tendrils of maternity reach from the pages, and she wondered whether her mother would ever know what *letting go* meant. As she put the book back and began to push the table against the wall, her hand touched the handle of a shallow drawer which was normally pressed to invisibility against the wall. She pulled the rosebud knob. Inside was a small black book with *Diary* in block letters on the cover. Although she knew her mother's modesty (she had never seen her with less on than a slip or a night gown) her curiosity pulled her to look into her mother's naked mind.

She leafed through pages until the words *"half born"* drew her attention:

"Dream: so strange, so real. I had something between my legs, half born. I tried to make it come, but it would not. And I tried to walk, to get away. But I could not move, and I could not get it out, and I could not see what it was."

Phyllis leafed through the diary trying to relate what she had just read to the mother she knew. Her mother had recorded only dreams. Phyllis puzzled over such a break with the controlled veneer her mother displayed to the world. Flashing to her, as she replaced the diary in its drawer: *the guilt of wound-*

ing her son's brain! What a weight she had taken on herself! Yet a difficult birth could hardly have been her fault, and it might not even have caused Arthur's cerebral palsy. Did desire to control lead to an overall rigidity?—or was it the other way around? The questions outweighed her guilt over reading her mother's diary and confused her brain as she pushed the table with its hidden drawer tight against the wall.

VI

July, 1943

No one in the house had time to admire the sun-drenched colors of early summer. Mrs. Dean had been home from the hospital for eight days and was still bedridden. Mary had been dividing her time between Arthur and Mrs. Dean who had been, as Phyllis said, complaining in her *heroic style*. "This discomfort is so very difficult to bear," she murmured, her face contracted in pain. But when Mary offered her an analgesic, she refused saying, "It jumbles my mind too horribly." She asked Mary for books to divert her attention from the pain, then there were more complaints. *"Bleak House* is just too heavy. Please get me a slim volume of poetry, Keats or Browning." Mary went back downstairs to the library. Next the drinking water was too warm, and she took the water bottle to the kitchen for ice.

Mary set the bottle on Mrs. Dean's bedside table and was about to return to Arthur's room. Mrs. Dean detained her saying, "I have something I would like to discuss with you and Phyllis. Would you please call her here."

The two girls stood together waiting for what they were certain would be bad news.

"I understand that you have been taking Arthur down into the garden."

Their simultaneous nods cut into the glum atmosphere.

"I really cannot allow you to do that."

"I don't see the harm," Phyllis said. "He enjoys it so much, these beautiful warm days…"

"You know what I think about exposing him to the stares of strangers, Phyllis. Anyone who walks along the sidewalk can stare over the garden fence. And children can tease with such cruelty."

"Really, Mother, I don't think…"

"This is my wish. You already know my reasons." She dismissed them. "Now I really must rest. These altercations are extremely difficult for me."

Phyllis did not know how to salvage the truncated conversation. She left the room wondering whether her mother was as sure of her decisions as she pretended to be. Or did she need to be so rigid to protect her self-image as the perfect mother to Arthur?

●

During the long days, Mary grabbed time for herself wherever she could find it, usually in Arthur's room. "I've got stuff I've got to get off my chest," Mary said. "Okay with you if I write a letter?"

"You—talk—to—me?"

But she didn't want to tell him what it was. She wrote her letter. Arthur watched her finish, then lick the flap. Her tongue was pink and kittenish.

"Tell—where—you—live."

Mary's attention shifted slowly away from the letter she had been absorbed in composing. After checking the long number after the lieutenant's name on the envelope, Mary pushed her letter aside and concentrated on Arthur's question. "Where I live now? It's in a real old apartment that used to be a carriage house back when they had horses. I room with my friend, Celeste. She's a nurse in the enormous mansion that's been converted to a nursing home and a school for special people like you. Celeste and I painted all the walls and did the floors in our carriage house, so it looks like new. Best of all, I've got a spunky kitten. Today is Friday, so I can go home for the weekend and play with her."

"You—have—home—here."

"Sort of. But not a home for Snow White."

"I—want—you—to—bring—her."

"A cat! With your mother home? Never!"

"This—is—my—room."

"Your room..." Anger tensed Mary's face.

"You're—mad. Me?"

"Oh, Arthur, no! I wish it really was your room, not..." Mary leaned over the arm of Arthur's chair and kissed his cheek, then hurried from the room as though to prevent Arthur from hearing the end of her angry sentence. But she said it out loud, and Arthur heard, "a cage."

She likes me, and she takes me out. He was making a soft tone in his throat as Mary walked up the ramp.

Arthur hated saying *good bye* to Mary on Friday afternoons. The bus connections were poor, so, as usual, Carl would drive her to her apartment, then Mr. Dean would pick her up on Sunday night.

●

It had been a long Sunday full of Mrs. Dean's heroic complaints. Arthur had been lost in some private dream world.

Phyllis was furious with her art teacher who refused to give her a critique on her "self-portrait as an animal" assignment because she had refused to answer any questions about it. "It is essential that you identify your subjects so as to clarify the interpretation. I can't evaluate your work without knowing whether your execution is appropriate to your concept." Phyllis had walked out of the class as she formed an unspeakable response: *You are not going to dissect me! I am an artist, not a guinea pig.*

Her grandiose pronouncement, private though it was, fueled Phyllis's fear of failure in her artistic struggles. Snatches of scenes formed patterns and textures in her mind, but they all fell short of her lofty dreams. All day the twists and turns of her baroque brain conceived of projects too complex to undertake.

When she went into Arthur's room hoping to find a sympathetic ear, some help toward a strong, gripping image, even the radio was mute. Arthur was deep in his own thoughts.

When evening came and it was time to go for Mary, both Phyllis and her father were eager to escape from the house. As Mrs. Dean was still spending most of her time in bed, his father wheeled Arthur to her room and left him close beside his mother. Should she need help in caring for him, she could ring for Carl's wife, Ilie, who was in the kitchen.

"It's strange to see Arthur away from his room," her father said to Phyllis as he pulled out of the driveway.

"Always in his room. Time is so monotonous for Arthur!" Phyllis exclaimed. "In his room, in his room, in his room—until the last two weeks."

"Your mother thought it best."

Mother and her little boxes! People boxes tied up with string. All labeled. You're ignoring the last two weeks as if they never happened, as if you haven't even seen what Mary and I've been doing for Arthur, struggling down the garden steps with his chair and up again. Phyllis found her voice: "I suppose she always knows what's best for Arthur?" *And for me.*

He ignored the barbs in Phyllis's question. "You know the story. The doctor considered it best." He concentrated on a left turn.

"But what about Arthur? What's best for him? It was his doctor, but he wasn't the one who went doctor shopping. She gets to make all our choices."

He was silent for a long time, his eyes fixed on the road ahead. "Phyllis, you may think your mother books up your life calendar, but there's always room for choice, if you're smart enough to work for it."

"I guess I'm in a bad mood," Phyllis said, "but…" She left the sentence hanging as she returned to her own thoughts. *If Mother was the mother of spring, would she hold the buds tight in the dark of her hand?* Buds escaping from a fist—Phyllis began to see possibilities for an image she could paint.

As they passed the railroad depot, Phyllis looked beyond the confines of the car to the soldiers and sailors dotting the steps, forming nuclear centers with bright civilian cells moving around them. *Are the circles just family boxes?*

Phyllis stared at the gas rationing sticker on the lower corner of the windshield; the thick black A meant limited mobility. Her thoughts—the goldfish in her mind swimming in tight circles. Her father was silent, face expressionless. Two bowls; two lonely fish. But if they were released, would they know how to swim away straight? Her mother kept her fish in separate bowls and shook in just a little carefully measured food.

Phyllis cut into the silence. "I suppose it isn't very nice of me to feel so irritated with Mother, but she treats Arthur like a fragile thing to be packed away in excelsior"—She recalled her mother's diary—or hidden like something sinful, a failed effort to give birth.

"Sometimes I feel like that too, but with obligations instead of excelsior."

"Oh?" She was feeling guilty pricks and only half listened to her father.

"Don't you?" he asked.

Phyllis realized she had been thinking of obligations, but only to herself.

"Phyllis, she's completely loyal to her family, and in her own way she loves us very much, just as much as she possibly can." He added hesitantly, "whatever we do."

"But…" Her father waited while she put her thoughts together. "It's as if she was pulling me out of the ground and then just hanging onto the roots with both her hands."

"Love in an open hand?" He shook his head. "It takes courage to love someone that way."

As the car moved from the walled tunnels of downtown and past lower structures, Phyllis remembered her childhood image of her father: tall protector with a scratchy face, reliable as furniture, yet feared and unapproachable. Was it her mother who had kept him so removed from her world? If that was it, she had one more thing to blame her for. Phyllis recalled her father in his business suit, an isolated man at the corner desk in the living room or in his den, smoothly dealing out his cards for solitaire. But at BAYLIS & DEAN with its clean smell of gun oil and new canvas, he was a different man—speaking with enthusiastic authority in answer to customers' questions that sprang from intent minds and excited emotions. Then, in his corner office at the back of the store, she vividly recalled his roll-top desk with moose antlers spread above it. On the only bare wall was a painting of seals basking on an iceberg, relaxed as sunbathers. "I like that picture in your office," she said abruptly.

"Yes." His affectionate smile puzzled Phyllis. "You were a unique little girl, standing in command of that chair like a pilot at the helm of his ship. Yet often you were so shy."

"No, I don't mean the one of me standing on the chair. I mean the painting on the wall by the door, the one of seals on the iceberg."

His face warmed with a deep but transient smile. "Marsha gave me that—before she was married."

Again Phyllis's memory took her back: Pearl Harbor, then the incongruous sequel: *A Midsummer Night's Dream* with big warm Marsha sitting in the car beside her father. Then the memory of her mother's choked sobs that seemed to put steel bands around her anger or her grief.... Phyllis turned off the memory, wanting to keep her father and Marsha behind their curtain of privacy.

They drove down a quiet street held under the arms of old elms. The car coasted and stopped silently in front of the remodeled carriage house behind the refurbished Victorian home topped with cupolas and trimmed with intricate gingerbread.

Mary was kneeling on the grass in front of the carriage house, her small suitcase beside her; but she did not see them drive up. She was bent over her kitten, a ball of white fluff that lay on its back batting her hair with a soft forepaw. Mary was laughing too hard to hear them until they called.

The drive home was animated with lighthearted chatter.

"Timmy says my kitty cat is 'our *kiddy* cat'," Mary said. "We're real anxious to have kids."

"*Timmy? Kids?* Then you're going to be married?" Mr. Dean questioned.

"Yes. Right after the war. Or maybe before," Mary answered. "It's real hard to wait without seeing him."

"Yes, I'm sure it is. Congratulations to you, to both of you."

Phyllis knew this, but she had postponed telling Arthur.

●

Arthur watched and watched. His caterpillar hung to a stick by its tail. It was days. One morning the bright stripes had darkened. That day it squirmed around, and Arthur felt his body squirming too. It wiggled and wiggled until the old skin split. Underneath was bright green like a jewel. The skin was a little dried up crumb by its tail. But it was Saturday, and Mary had gone home, so she wasn't with him to see it happen.

Sunday night Arthur watched his jade-green jewel, hanging like a big drop, until Mary came. He showed her. Now it was even prettier; there was a black line and little gold dots on the green, as shiny as real gold.

Mary leaned close to the jar. "What a jewel!" she exclaimed with an enthusiastic laugh. "I want to wear it around my neck—a jade pendent!"

Arthur stared as though his eyes—for her—could transform it. Then his attention shifted to a more likely possibility. "Tomorrow—I—want—to—go—outside."

Mary stood up with her lips pressed tightly together. "I'll be back in a few minutes." She went away quickly, the way she did when she got mad. When she came back he asked her again if he could go out.

Mary said, "No. There's no good reason. That's why I'm mad about it."

Monday morning he asked again, and Mary answered in a voice with sharp edges. "Your ma told me we can't."

"Why?"

Mrs. Dean's words were all but audible under Mary's, "No good reason. I already told you that." She was mad, but Arthur could tell she wasn't mad at him.

Arthur listened to Mary. "People live in their own skins without giving it a thought. Then they get this crazy idea that you're different, so you can't live in yours."

Arthur kept his face still, but his eyes searched Mary's face.

"Arthur, can you tell me? What bugs you the most? How cerebral palsy keeps you down or how people treat you?"

"You—treat—me—right. I—want—the—whole—world—to—treat—me—right."

"Then would you be okay—with C.P.?"

"No. I—want—to—walk. Then—I—could—be—a—man. Then—I—could—get—married."

Arthur watched Mary. She was looking out the window with her eyes far away.

Her skin is soft. I touch her gently, and I love her the way they say, 'in sickness and in health, till death do us part.' I love her all the time.

After a long silence, "I—want—to—go—out—of—the—dark," he said. "I—want—to—be—a—romantic—man."

●

When the dinner dishes were done, Mary went to her room. Phyllis followed up the back steps, avoiding the living room where her parents were listening to the radio: depressing news from some obscure Pacific island. She hated the thought of George being there. *"Better to have loved and lost…"* she wondered. It didn't seem good for George. He wanted to be so heroic, but he wrote about how homesick he was, and then he wrote, "I try to forget you by playing ping pong." She smiled through her regrets.

The music from Arthur's radio stopped her in the hall. *"There'll be bluebirds over the white cliffs of Dover…"* She hadn't thought about George for a long time. The song's strains of sad hope roused emotions she thought she had forgotten, and she wiped tears from her eyes with the back of her hand. She had been so unrealistic back then. Expecting George to rescue her from her mother's prison. She smiled through her tears. Some vision out of *The Arabian Nights*. Maybe he expected it too.

Mary was so happy with Timmy—one more thing to envy. Phyllis was drawn to the third floor.

Mary's door was open. Phyllis had scarcely been in the room since Edie left it so many years ago. Now the green wicker table reminded Phyllis of Eagle's cage, and she felt the warmth of Edie in this room that was now Mary's. She wanted to let Mary know the history. "This is..." Phyllis began, but Mary was deep in her own serious thoughts, and Phyllis broke off.

"So much room in this house!" Mary exclaimed, "But no space feels like mine. I'm sorry, but I feel so bossed, sometimes I get too mad to keep still. It's all I can do to shut up in front of Arthur. Last Friday I just had to tell him about your ma. I didn't want him blaming me for keeping him locked up."

"That's okay. I feel the same way, sort of," Phyllis said.

"But you're used to it. For me it's real different. Your mom, she wants me to treat Arthur like blown glass."

Phyllis smiled at the image. "I know. The only person I knew—before you—who treated him like a real person was Edie."

"Edie! Oh my God! Edie who? I know a woman named Edie."

Mary's vehemence puzzled Phyllis, and her voice raised in a question mark. "A nurse we had a long time ago? Edie Markson? She lived up here."

"Small world department! Was she Indian?" Mary gave Phyllis time only for a quick nod. "I had her for a teacher in nursing school, massage. She was a blast. So much new stuff. Part of it she got from some medicine woman, not when she was growing up, but later. Some of us went to her apartment, and that's where she taught us about shamanism. Like she was giving us a whole way to see the world."

"Father told me she scared Mother," Phyllis said.

"I bet! She's really powerful, and she must have seen right into your mother. Mrs. Dean would have hated that!"

"Yes, she's really private."

"I suppose she's got stuff she wants to forget. Guess we all do. A lot of my past life I wanted to just erase." Mary paused. "I told Edie about some of the stuff. Then she said 'no, remember it all. Your life knows what it's doing; it makes your body a vase full of memories that must not be spilled.' The way she said it, it makes me keep thinking about it."

Phyllis wanted to ask her about those memories, but, afraid that Mary would object to her prying, Phyllis stood beside her in silence hoping that she would say more. They were looking at the same view from Mary's room that Phyllis had from hers, but from higher up. The low sun caught the dark super-structure of the bridge across the Mississippi over a mile away. The delicate span looked like a toy. "I used to live near there, a long time ago," Mary said.

"I know that place!" Phyllis's words raced with excitement at finding another link to Mary. "We used to go down to the river for my landscape class when I was in high school."

Phyllis remembered watching the water, deep and black as though it should be dead, but it was alive and moving, playing with little bits of wood and dirty papers, and where it flowed thin over a shallow rock, it showed satin swirls of oiled blues and copper greens. Behind it, the bridge grew suddenly out of the rocky ground and over the dark water, like some kind of temple rising on great round concrete columns.

Phyllis followed Mary to her brass bed, and they sat on the edge of it. "When I lived there," Mary said, "there was a twisting dirt path beside the river, and just before we got to it, there was a bakery. The fresh bread smelled so good! A man used to knead the dough on a floury wood table, and the hairs on his arms got powdered with it. He'd give us sweepings from the slicer."

"Sweepings?" Phyllis prodded, but Mary remained silent,

and Phyllis tried again. "When you've lived in a place, it must be funny to see it from so far up and away—a different experience to put in the vase."

"Yeah. It seems so big when you're under it. Like the whole city's on top of you." Mary put her hands to her ears. "The trucks really make a rumble."

"I painted those pillars once when our art class went down there. They look strong enough to hold the world."

"The pigeons think it's a great big bird cage, and they shit the stones white.—(sorry, I shouldn't say that, but that's what my brothers always said.) The pigeons get real tame 'cause we throw them crumbs from the bakery. But the boys throw stones at them, and sometimes they kill one."

As Mary spoke, Phyllis fantasized her as an incongruous Florence Nightingale standing on a rock under the dark bridge in her nurse's cap and uniform with pigeons flying all around her, she scattering crumbs and chasing away stone-throwing boys.

"Real noisy!" Mary exclaimed, "Like echoes when they fly!"

Suddenly Phyllis heard the brittle sound of wind, loud in their pinion feathers. She looked across the bed at Mary grasping the foot rail of her bed and leaning her chin in her hands. "What are you thinking?"

"I was remembering something, something my father told me once...before he died." Mary paused for a long time, and her eyes were wet, but no tears spilled over her lids. She continued. "I haven't thought of it for ages. After Pa died, I told my little brother what he said. 'If you tie a wish to a bird's wing, your wish will come true.' I didn't tell my brother it was one of Pa's jokes. Then little Johnny wrote a wish on a piece of paper. He got a piece of string, and he came down here..."

"Here?" Phyllis questioned.

"Guess I feel like I'm back under that bridge." Mary laughed. "Johnny was so proud when he told me. He'd tied his wish to a wing all right. The wing of a dead bird."

"A dead bird..." Phyllis felt an impulse to hug Mary, but

Mary looked as though she was too wrapped in her own thoughts. Yet Phyllis was drawn to make a connection. "You're my best friend," she said. But Phyllis felt the echoing rumble of traffic all over her words, rolling them flat.

After Pa died. Mary had said it so casually. Her mother alone? Not enough money? All that stayed under the bridge, and Phyllis felt no invitation to intrude into Mary's life.

Phyllis had given up the thought of Mary responding to her proffered friendship when Mary abruptly asked, "What? Oh, you're my friend too." Mary smiled at her, but Phyllis missed the intensity from Mary that she felt herself. "But sometimes we're just too different," Mary added.

Feeling emotionally clumsy, Phyllis raked her fingers up through her hair, then said—trying to make it sound casual, "It's good to have you here."

"Yeah," Mary said halfheartedly.

After a silence Phyllis didn't know how to fill, she got up off the bed. "Guess I'll be going." She walked toward the door knowing she was a superfluous adjunct to Mary's life.

Mary turned on her radio, and the strains of "In the Mood" from Glenn Miller's big band followed Phyllis down the stairs, but Mary's mood had left her out.

●

Two days later Mary told Mrs. Dean that she was leaving. One of the nurses who worked at the nursing home had gone into the army, and Mary agreed to fill the position. "It'll be real convenient," she told Phyllis, "living right next to work. I thought of going into the army too, but sure as Timmy comes home on leave, I'd be in Europe or else in the Pacific stuck on some palm-tree island."

Phyllis told Arthur. For a long time he responded only with startled contractions until, finally, he could speak. "I—need— to—do—something."

"What's that?"

"I—love—somebody—who—is—going—away."

"I know."

"I—think—my—mind—is—cuckoo."

"No!"

Arthur overrode Phyllis's objection. "because—every—time—I—see—her—I—see—an—angel. I—don't—know—what—to—do. I—worry. My—feeling—for—her—is—really—down—deep. But—I—know—that—I—can't—make—my—arms—go—all—around—her. But—I—can't-go—on—feeling—like—this."

"Have you told her? Sometimes it helps to talk about it—maybe."

"I—don't—know—how."

Phyllis hoped that, somehow, Mary could find a way to help him get his feelings out. She suggested a letter to her.

He wrote:

> *Dear Mary,*
> *I don't want you to go away from here. I've got a problem.*
> *I can't go with you.*
> *I don't know what I am going to do with my life.*
> *A star was born one day. Her name is Mary.*

He jerked in frustration as Phyllis signed his name, folded the paper and put it in his pocket. Her head was shaking as much as his. "You can give it to her at supper."

As Phyllis got up to leave, Arthur tried to speak. She heard the sounds, but the meaning cleared only after she had left him: "If I'm such a burden, why was I born?"

She went back to him and shouted, "No. We love you, and you teach us a lot."

●

The very next day—*Mary gone. My whole life gone.* His tree couldn't help; it only shook oak leaves. Phyllis came, at first it didn't matter. Then she said, "I've got news for you."

It didn't matter until he heard her name.

"Mary asked us over, you and me and father. She asked us for lunch, 'I'm warning you, real simple' she said. And she's going to show you the nursing home where she's going to work with people in wheel chairs, like you. It's okay. Father said so, but Mother's still too weak to come."

●

Long waiting for the day. After breakfast Phyllis helped Arthur get dressed. "You can wear your new suit," she said. "It's the one Mother got before she went to the hospital—when she thought you had to go to a nursing home."

Then Phyllis had to leave him to do chores. Arthur heard her shout, "Why? Just tell me why I have to scour the sink and wash the bathroom floor...*every* day."

Arthur heard his mother in the hall when she told Phyllis, "I am not sure you should have accepted that girl's invitation."

"She's not 'that girl.' She's Mary."

"Yeaa—" Arthur agreed, although Phyllis couldn't hear him.

Phyllis came back with their father. Arthur twisted in his chair to greet them. His mouth stretched wide, his arms and legs jerked. His father tied his tie. Then they shook hands. "That's a good-looking suit there, young fellow!"

Arthur had not yet given Mary his letter, and Phyllis put it in his breast pocket. "You can give it to her at lunch," she said.

His father gathered Arthur in his arms—willing spirit reaching out; body poking and jerking, its parts moving in opposition. Phyllis wheeled the empty chair down the front steps.

Their mother watched them from an upstairs window as his father lifted Arthur into the car. Phyllis knelt on the front seat behind the wheel and pulled Arthur's legs straight. She stayed beside him, her arm around his shoulders, to hold him upright on the seat. He flailed his arms, and he was talking; but even if he had something important to say, he was too excited to make himself understood.

Arthur's exuberance flashed through his limbs like the joys of separate children, and Phyllis had a hard time keeping him from falling against the door or forward to the windshield.

As they drove away, Mrs. Dean's brave smile followed as though it were extended to them on a rubber band. Then, just as Phyllis felt it snap, her father said, "Your mother would like to be with us."

"I think she would feel awkward. I know Mary would."

"I suppose she would."

"Yeah—"

"Arthur agrees, and I'm sure he's right," Phyllis said.

The car crunched to a stop in the small gravel parking area between the remodeled carriage house and the main house, sparkling with new white paint. Mary stood at the door of the nursing home waiting to greet them. "You do look handsome all dressed up."

"Yeaa—" Arthur responded.

"Aren't you pleased with yourself," his father teased.

Arthur laughed as he fell from the car into his father's arms and was lifted into his chair. Mary took the handles, expertly navigating the frost-heaved sidewalk blocks.

The door opened to sounds of an out-of-tune piano, a cacophony of human voices, and Mary's explanation, "It's singing time." Although Phyllis scarcely recognized "Home on the Range," the song stirred her emotion beyond anything she could account for by what she saw, heard, or understood.

Phyllis puzzled over these emotions as she followed Mary's tour, her mind busy with images to be painted in memory and repainted over time: the large windows framed by flowered chintz curtains fluttering over the plants that cluttered the sills, Mary's long tanned legs swinging past wheels of glittering chrome, a half-circle of slumped residents, their chairs around an upright piano.

What Phyllis felt was joy, clean, uncomplicated by any strain toward musical results; joy kicking up like spray from happy children in a wading pool or puppies racing on the lawn. She was with people who had no responsibility for hammering out "better lives" and teachers who had no obligation to manufacture socially dictated behaviors to fit some preordained expectations. What Phyllis sensed, but did not yet know, was that the flow of unguarded feeling in the small group was what made the free play with "the deer and the antelope" possible. It was what she caught in her heart but could not yet understand with her head.

Phyllis focused on a dark-haired girl slumped, limp and heavy, in her chair. She was about Arthur's age, arms floating uncontrolled, singing in wide-mouthed enthusiasm. Saliva bubbled down her chin, and a strand of hair was stuck to the corner of her mouth. Phyllis saw the whole image, but it was the enthusiasm, like the grin of the vanishing Cheshire cat, which remained with her.

A boy (or a man) was facing the wall where his chair was jammed against the side of a desk. Phyllis noticed only his arm, so like Arthur's, down stiffly, fingers like a fork's long tines, reaching between the spokes of his wheel. "Aahh—" Arthur said.

"You know what that feels like, don't you, Arthur?" Mary noted, looking over her shoulder as she went to free the boy's fingers from the spokes of the wheel.

"Aahh—" Arthur watched Mary with intense concentration as she stroked the boy's shoulder, "David, David." Over and over she repeated his name, over and over the same hypnotic song. Gradually his arm relaxed, and she freed his fingers, laying his hand in his lap and turning his chair away from the desk.

As though Arthur was hearing his own name, the magnet of Mary's voice drew him forward in his chair. Phyllis wheeled him after Mary who was taking David to the near-by window. Arthur was speaking softly, almost inaudibly. Phyllis could only guess at the repeated word: *Mary, Mary.* They watched her standing by a plant-festooned window, her head beside a large red flower almost as big as her face.

"Wow, what an amaryllis!" Mary exclaimed.

Arthur tried, "I—give—you—that—flower."

Mary smiled at him. "I'll remember it's from you," she said. "Now it's time to go to my house for lunch."

When Phyllis wheeled him outside, Mary came rushing toward Phyllis. "I got an exciting call last night. Long distance."

Arthur was listening. "I—don't—like—that," he muttered as Phyllis pushed him across the parking lot to Mary's apartment.

They entered a big room with a kitchen screened off by a burlap curtain decorated with multicolored yarns pulled through it. The first thing Mary did was to put Snow White on Arthur's lap. "I know you want to meet my kitty," she said as Arthur smiled widely.

Phyllis breathed in the rich smells of Mary's cooking, then followed her to the kitchen and watched her pull fragrant chicken pot pies from the oven, done just as they walked in the door.

As Mary put the lunch on the table, Phyllis and her father watched Snow White bat Arthur's tie with a pink and white paw. Phyllis squatted beside Arthur. "Have you given Mary your letter yet?"

He shook his head and began to speak as Mary returned with a towel to protect Arthur's suit. "This should do it." Phyllis started to help Mary tuck it under Arthur's collar, then drew back, catching Arthur's disappointment at his sister's intervention.

They pulled their chairs up to a round table with a yellow cloth. They raved about the golden-crusted pies served in individual ramekins. "It's just plain old chicken pie, another one of those meat-saving casseroles," Mary said, sitting next to Arthur so that she could feed him. "It's hot. You better blow on it." Phyllis noticed the rise in his chest; his breath control appeared to be improving.

"It's not like anything I ever tasted before," Phyllis said.

"It's good to see Arthur enjoying his food so much." His father reached into his pocket. "I nearly forgot; we brought you some ration stamps, meat and sugar. We don't want you to run short because of us."

"Thanks, Celeste and I can use them! Say, Arthur, don't give it all to Snow White!" The kitten attacked a corner of pie crust with her paw. "It's no mouse. It won't run."

Mary put a bowl of fruit on the table in a square of sunlight from the window, and the ordinary apples, pears and grapes were turned into a dramatically lighted still life.

Their plates were empty; the kitten was purring in Arthur's lap. Then, abruptly, Mary stood up. "It's nearly two o'clock already!" She took some glasses and hurried to the kitchen. In response to Mary's distracted fluster, Phyllis and her father rose quickly to their feet.

"Yes," Mr. Dean said. "We should be on our way. His mother will be wanting Arthur home."

Mary's "You must come again," sounded distracted.

Phyllis leaned over Arthur's chair. "The time went so fast! I know you don't want to go." His head was bent low over the kitten. "Do you want to give Mary your letter?" Phyllis retrieved it from his breast pocket and handed it to Mary as Arthur tried to pat the kitten, missed and jabbed at his own leg.

"Here, let me help." Phyllis opened Arthur's hand, fitting his fingers around the kitten's neck and shoulders as Mary watched. "Now you can feel how soft she is."

"Don't you two look happy!" As Mary spoke, the screen door banged, and she wheeled toward the gun-crack sound.

A deep voice shouted, "Surprise!"

"Timmy!" His energy swelled through the room, and all heads turned as Mary ran into the arms of the giant air force lieutenant, so tall the ceiling seemed to rest on his shoulders as he bent over her.

Voices jumbled in excited greetings. Laughter muffled words, and only the kitten's sharp scream managed to cut through with a separate voice.

Mary's arms reached up around Timmy's neck to his tawny G.I. cut. Her stretch revealed a small corner of Arthur's unread letter poking from her pocket. Then Phyllis focused on the gleam of Mary's diamond as she heard Arthur's screech swell in place of the kitten's voice, now silent. She mentally recited Arthur's letter as she watched Timmy's hand caress the hair Arthur so often stroked with his thoughts.

Arthur was bent low, knees up, back curved forward, head dropped toward his clenched right hand: an iron fetus. Three red lines were drawn in blood across the back of his hand. Phyllis's whole attention was pulled with Arthur's to the kitten's head, tongue protruding, terrified eyes bubbled out from her skull. Timmy got there first, his muscular hands over Arthur's, grappling with the vice-like grip. "Let go, goddamn, what are you trying to do? Kill him?"

"Timmy, no!" Mary was beside them. "Arthur can't help it. He didn't mean to. He just can't open his hands!"

Timmy shrank back, stammering like a child. "What? Sorry, God I'm sorry. Guess I've been triggering on reflex too long. Seeing that poor kitten, I guess I just lost it...." He put his thick hand gently on Arthur's shoulder, then stepped back toward the door.

Mary took Arthur's hand, softly helping until his wire fingers were free of the kitten. It gave one trembling shudder and was still. Arthur's scratched hands were smeared with blood. His body was contracted in one big fist of horror, and his sobs burst out in grating rasps. Phyllis, crouching beside him, watched a tear squeeze through one clenched eyelid and hang there as their father took the dead kitten off his lap. Mary rushed to take it and hold it to her breast. She tried all she knew to revive it, but to no avail.

Phyllis saw the quick action unravel in slow motion, Mary bringing warm water, washing Arthur's hands and putting a dressing on the scratches while useless words fell on the disaster. His father carried Arthur to the car. Mary and Timmy stood still and silent behind the car.

●

They don't take me to the bathroom. I can't ask.

Mary hates me. I can't tell her I'm sorry. She can't hear me say 'love.'

Arthur stared at Timmy while Phyllis put the chair into the trunk. Timmy was bent over Mary, and his arms were around her so that Arthur could hardly see her. *He thinks he's so big and tough he can do anything. He makes me small until I am nothing, and he makes Mary small too. I hate hate hate him.* Arthur's hard-focused gaze put blood on Timmy's neck—like the polar bear—blood all around. That man dead; not Snow White. "Ahh—" Nobody heard. They pushed him to the middle of the front seat. One foot caught on the gear shift, one knee pressed against it. His father was behind the wheel.

Lips parted, silent, Mary looked at Arthur.

She doesn't talk to me.

On the way home their father talked about the lunch.

Arthur was immersed in his own problem. *I don't want to listen. I just try to hold it.*

When they got home, it was still okay. But when his father took him, his legs caught at the gear shift again. They caught at the edge of the seat and they caught at the door. Some leaks out. *I can't wait.*

●

Their father exclaimed as he took Arthur into his arms; at the same time, as Phyllis was pulling Arthur's chair out of the trunk, she heard his moan that could have been, "Sorry." When she came around to the passenger door, Phyllis caught the acrid smell of urine. "We forgot to take Arthur to the bathroom!"

His father laughed. "Come on, Arthur. After all, we never gave you a chance. Remember, all you have to save you is your..." The word *laughter* jammed in his throat.

Phyllis followed them into the house anticipating her mother's questions and hoping it would work out to leave them to her father.

"Shh," he said as he carried Arthur upstairs. "We'll get you all cleaned up before your mother finds out."

Phyllis stayed with Arthur while their father changed, then she laid out clean clothes while the men were in the bathroom. Phyllis saw for the first time how able her father was in caring for Arthur.

Mrs. Dean heard the water running in the tub. "What is going on?"

Instead of answering, Phyllis closed herself in her room.

The afternoon dragged on until finally it was supper time. "What do you want us to have?" Phyllis asked her mother.

She put her book on the bedside table and answered indecisively, "I believe waffles are quite simple."

On her way to the kitchen Phyllis realized: *I believe...* So her mother had never made them!

While standing in the middle of the wide white floor, Phyllis thought back to the days of Hilda. Again she became a child sitting at the kitchen table. The polished waffle iron, the creamy thick...what do they call it? *Dough* was for bread. The thick creamy pour had sizzled onto the hot iron. Then, watching the top rise up, the color, the taste... Then she had been hungry, now the day's disaster turned her stomach against food.

After finding *waffels* in the cook book, Phyllis searched the shelves for the ingredients. She pulled the flour sack off the upper shelf. Disaster—flour dusted over her head and drifted to the floor. White tracks to the table to put down the flour sack. White tracks to the sink. White tracks to the broom closet to get the scrub pail, then back again. She'd have to wash the whole floor! She tossed her head in exasperation, and the flour from her hair got into her eyes.

Phyllis sat down on the floor bent double with sobs. Why now? The smallest disaster of the day. She checked herself just as she was about to rub more flour into her eyes with a floury fist. She went to the sink, washed her hands and face. Next the floor. The flour paste left gray streaks on the white tiles. *I don't care.* She went back to her waffle making and dumped everything in the bowl together. She stirred the lumpy mess, knowing that she would never get it right.

It took forever for the little red arrow on the waffle iron to point to ON. She poured the liquid in. Thick yellow drips of juice ran all down the shiny side. But the sizzling sounded good, the top rose up. Finally it was quiet, and steam stopped coming from the sides.

Phyllis lifted. It didn't come, and she pulled harder. It opened, but the waffle was split in two, stuck both top and bottom. She might have wept again, but she heard steps from the pantry. "How is it coming?" Her father's voice, his step, everything so cheerful! "They smell great."

Mutely she pointed.

"Looks like somebody washed the grease off. That's no way to treat an iron!" He took it to the sink, picked with a knife and scrubbed with a wire brush. "Good enough. Now we'll try with grease, lots of it."

Phyllis's load of misery left no room for food. She watched her father spread the butter and pour on the syrup. Through a mouthful of paste he exclaimed, "These are swell!"

"I'm sorry, Father. I just can't eat. But thanks for helping."

"It's been a rough day," he said as he got a plate ready for his wife.

Phyllis took the waffle upstairs to her mother, then went to her room.

●

The next day Arthur was waiting for the long morning to go by, alone with his thoughts. *Soon Timmy will go away into the war. Maybe his airplane will crash.*

Arthur looked out at the steel sky, heat and humidity meeting in a miserable suffocating embrace. Dead Snow White, and no way to help Mary. No way to tell her he was sorry. He could reach out and touch her cheek gently so she could feel he loved her—happening only in his own head. He felt like the heavy day full of rain that would not fall, his passion squeezed into loneliness. *If I could get out*— He waited for Phyllis to come so he could tell her. She came.

"I—want—to—live—in—Mary's—place. Mary—will—help—me—talk. Then—everyone—will—know—who—I—am."

Phyllis saw his determination so strong that it surrounded him like a spotlight. "I'll call Mother," she said, trying to believe that Arthur's adult assertion would be a match for their mother's tiger-like possession of her cub.

Mrs. Dean was lying on her chase lounge, delicate rose buds against a background of pale gray that was the same shade, but darker than her face. She put down her book.

"Do you feel up to coming to Arthur's room for a few minutes? He has something important to ask you."

Phyllis waited as her mother put the volume of Emily Dickenson's poems on the little table beside her chaise. Phyllis offered her arm, and her mother leaned heavily as she rose to her feet.

Phyllis walked behind her mother, noticing how slowly and painfully she moved and how carefully her feet, in their narrow shoes, pointed outward.

They stood in front of Arthur's chair. She told her mother Arthur's words.

"But that's impossible!"

"Mother! Are you blind and deaf?"

She countered Phyllis's emotion in tones tight with her frightened rationality. "It's just too great a risk to take. He would be just one more crippled boy in a room full of strangers. Now, especially, when nurses are so scarce. He simply would not get the care he is used to. And the risk of contagion... So great!"

"But Mother," She heard her voice, powerless, like a child's whine, but she must try. "You said Arthur shouldn't compare himself with 'normal' people." Phyllis held her fingers in quotation marks beside her face. "This would give him a chance to make friends who lead the kind of life he does. Don't you..."

"Dear Child..."

"No!" burst from Phyllis in a shout.

But her mother continued as though she had not heard. "The cream of our health workers are with our fighting men. Arthur has always been surrounded by refined people who are always ready to help him, and…"

"All those years with Miss Bitzer getting more senile by the minute!" Phyllis exclaimed.

Arthur's roars of protest stopped her mother's words, but her face was stiff with determination.

"Phyllis, that is not fair. She was completely loyal and con-scientious."

Hope wilted under the pall of their mother's fearful immutability, the marsupial with an iron pouch. She patted her boy, and then she gave him her decision. *"No."*

In the afternoon Arthur looked up at his ticking cuckoo clock. "I—want—to—write—a—story."

Phyllis gripped the pencil.

"The cuckoo clock said twelve o'clock. I'm sitting in my chair getting old. I'm looking out my window, and I see a big bar across the street. It has a big table with chairs around it. I go there. I want to forget everything, but I hear the jukebox. It's playing a tune, my favorite, and it happens to be my girl friend singing. It happens to be a sad song because my girl friend is gone to heaven. I don't know what to do, and I'm scared to look back in the past because all I see is her. All I see is her face. It can't be her because she's been dead ten years. If I decide to say all the good things about her, I will be here all week. If I don't let my mind think about her, it will hurt me. Then it will do the damndest things.

"If I do get loaded, I might drive myself up the wall. I feel like I'm going up the wall too many times. I don't want my girl friend to see me because if she does, she would feel hurt and let down. Who wants to see a drunk anyway?

"She looks down at me like an angel. She has white wings and blond hair and blue eyes, and she has a white cape and a long white dress. She says, 'Hi.'

"I say, 'Hi, Angel.'

"She took out a book, and she sang a poem. It was a prayer that said everything. I believed, but I don't know how I could believe in an angel. I hear a door opening just a crack. I could see Mary off in the wild blue yonder. I wish we could live our lives over and be together.

Phyllis's "Wild Blue Yonder" was the R.O.T.C. marching through her college campus singing the air force song. "Arthur, just what do you mean by 'wild blue yonder'?"

"It's—like—angels—all—over—you."

"What are angels? Like mothers or girlfriends or spirits or what?"

"Angels—are—like—souls. Like—us—in—a—way. They— come—from—the—sky—from—everywhere—and—they— get—everywhere."

"I guess I see them that way too. And what do you mean by 'wild'?"

"I—see—God—that's—where—God—is."

"Is anything else there?"

"Everything—the—wild—blue—is—love—and—hate— and—sometimes—murder. Everything—is—there."

"Like God writes a book," Phyllis mused, "and the first page is birth, and the last page is death, but I don't know about murder."

"Sometimes—it—should—happen."

Phyllis shook her head but knew that words would not touch the fury that held Arthur's small muscles in still tighter knots. She got up to rub his shoulders, his arms, and the part of his back she could reach. She turned his radio to a music station and left him with *"Saturday night is the loneliest night of the week..."*

VII

August, 1943

The summer days continued slow and flat and all the same.

As Arthur looked into Phyllis's face, his pleading look was intense. I—hurt—can—you—help."

"I don't see how. What do you mean?"

"Teach—me—like—Mary."

Uncomprehending, Phyllis shook her head.

"In—the—home. With—that—man."

"Oh, you mean the way she got that man's finger untangled from the spokes of his chair?"

"Yeah—like—that."

"Okay," Phyllis said. "I suppose we can try."

Arthur smiled. "I'm—just—a—mixed—up—puppet—with—strings—tied—wrong."

"Okay," she answered, smiling at his image. "Then what we have to do is untie all the nerve endings and let the puppet go limp and relaxed. But you're a lot more than a puppet!"

"Yeah—"

Phyllis sat quietly until doubts about her ability stopped rustling in her mind. Then, in a voice that was next to a whisper, she chanted his name, "Arthur," over and over and over. She saw his eyes close just before hers did.

Abruptly the vacuum cleaner roared from the hall. Arthur's body jerked violently, accompanied by an explosion of his voice that brought their mother to the top of the ramp. "My dear! What is it?"

"It's okay, Mother. It was just the vacuum cleaner starting suddenly. I jumped too."

"You did sound frightened; I am so glad it was nothing serious." She asked Arthur what he wanted for lunch, then left, and Phyllis started over.

This time it took Arthur longer to relax, and Phyllis was about to give up when, finally, the spasticity began to ease until his muscles became soft as in sleep, and she could move his limp arm.

The long slow practice continued through July and into August. Arthur's purpose was steady, and he learned to accept Phyllis's hypnotic voice more and more quickly.

●

Mary had been gone for six weeks. Their mother had given Arthur his bath and dressed him, their father had gotten Arthur into his chair, and Phyllis had finished feeding him his breakfast. He was sunk low in his chair.

"You look like a wilted dandelion, and I feel like that too." Phyllis turned her face to the fan and thought of snow. "Would it help to relax?"

"When—I—do—it—I—can't—move—and—when—I—move—I—get—too—tight."

"I guess that's how it has to be." She sat in the rocker. It creaked.

Finally he asked, "How—is—your—art?"

"I'm seeing a lot of new images, but then I can't get them out of my head. I don't want to try putting them on paper. They remind me of Edgar Allan Poe. Too morbid."

He gave an unintelligible sound, then avoided the effort of speech for a long time.

"Aw—ee—a—aaa—ou."

Two syllables in that last word: "*Draw me a*, but I don't get the rest."

"Ah—ou."

"I don't get it." His speech seemed to be regressing, and her energy for understanding regressed with it. He again repeated. It went on—that flow of undifferentiated vowels that tied Phyllis in knots of meaningless sound. The mosquito buzz of the fan sounded hot, and the air it stirred was hot too. She thought of ice, but it made her feel like a sponge soaked in her brother's troubles, then left in the snow to freeze. She shivered in spite of the heat.

Phyllis was about to leave Arthur alone with his frustration when she noticed he was turning his eyes toward a newspaper on top of the book case across the room. Phyllis got up, her skirt sticking to her legs, and brought the paper to him. Page by page she went through it until finally he stopped her at the comics on the last page. "Kids?" she questioned, noticing "The Katzenjammer Kids" at the bottom of the page. But Arthur's word had two vowel sounds. "I'm sorry." Arthur seemed excited. "That's it?" Phyllis was close but not there yet. "Children?"

Wrong again. Arthur's enthusiasm melted. "Hairbreath Harry?" she asked in a deadened voice. Again Arthur raised a little in his chair, his facial muscles taut.

Finally Phyllis put the two responses together. "Comics?" Again she was close. "Cartoon." Arthur's laugh was wide open. "You want me to draw you a cartoon!"

Arthur opened his mouth preparing to speak again. "Draw—a—nah—an—home."

"Just a minute: 'draw a,' but I don't get the next word. A something home?"

There were many repetitions before he switched words.

"Mary?" Phyllis watched his eyes. "But the word is longer?" Again he repeated the long word, and Phyllis made the connection with Mary. "Oh, *nursing home!* You want me to draw you a nursing home?—but a cartoon?"

"With—wings," he said.

"A nursing home with wings!" Arthur evoked his sister's long, long awaited laughter, but it was of relief.

"We—are—sad. I—wanted—a—cheer—us—up." Phyllis's laugh flattened over a hollow center.

"For—Mary."

Phyllis sat down at her desk intending to dash off a quick sketch to fit Arthur's cartoon. But she could not do it casually after Arthur had worked on his leaden joke for over an hour.

Arthur asked daily about his cartoon, but it took Phyllis nearly a week to get around to the drawing. She sketched conventional trees under the house which, propelled by a pair of stubby wings, soared at a cockeyed angle above the treetops. As an afterthought, she added a man in a winged wheelchair flying into his *wild blue yonder.*

Phyllis wanted to drive to Mary's apartment, but the errand was too frivolous a use for their A gas ration, so she mailed the drawing.

Mary called the day she received her cartoon. "Phyllis, what a job you two guys did! I showed it to the gang, and my guys loved it! We're getting it framed and then we're going to hang it up in the class room. Just the lift I need now with Timmy gone. Honest, he's more scared than I am! He tried not to let on, but I could tell. Pilots used to get a year's training, and now it's only eight months, and Timmy might go to Europe, and those German planes are *fast* and they dodge real quick. And on top of all that, I've gotta look for a new roommate. Celeste's getting a job in an army hospital. She doesn't know where yet. But I'm talking your ear off, and I really meant to talk to Arthur."

"I'm glad you told me all that news. Your life is so full, and just nothing happens around here. Of course Arthur misses you a whole lot, you know that. But I won't make him wait any longer. His first phone call!"

Phyllis whispered in Arthur's ear.

"I—talk—to—Mary!?"

"Yes, really. I'll help you." Phyllis wheeled him into the hall and leaned over the phone she held to his ear. Mary climaxed her thanks: "Can you go out for a walk with me some day soon?" His laughing words stumbled out inaudibly, but quickly following his joy, his body collapsed in on itself.

"What's the matter," Phyllis asked.

"Mother."

Phyllis took the phone. "Arthur's afraid Mother won't let him go, but I think we can find a way to work it out."

Phyllis agreed to "chaperone" Arthur's first date as he "walked" by the river with Mary. However, as the summer passed by, Mrs. Dean found constant reasons to postpone the trip. The leaves had turned gold by the time the day finally arrived. Predictably Mrs. Dean found another objection.

"Not today! I cannot spare you, Phyllis. I am going to have my poetry ladies for tea, and there is only Ilie to help. She has to leave at 3:30, so I was counting on you."

"But Mary can't take Arthur alone, and we've put it off too long already."

"I am sorry, it can not be helped. I never liked that idea anyway. So many people walk along the river road." She spread her hands in a helpless gesture, then exclaimed, "All the stares he would get! I cannot bear it."

Mrs. Dean was on her way to Arthur's room. Phyllis stood in the hall waiting for what she knew would happen. It started hard and suddenly. Arthur's screams filled the house, and Phyllis heard the banging as he kicked his stocking feet, then the howl as he thrust himself out of his chair.

Mrs. Dean forgot her weakness and clipped up the ramp, "What can I do?" she protested.

Phyllis translated for Arthur, now a heap on the floor. "Let—me—go."

On hearing Arthur's voice, Mrs. Dean lost her determination, and her face tensed in thought. "Let me think..." After a long pause, she said reluctantly, "Yes, I suppose Carl can drive Arthur and that aide to the river, then wait for them to finish their walk."

"Mary is not an aide. She is a *registered nurse,* and if she didn't hate hospital work, she wouldn't even have worked here!" Phyllis exclaimed.

It was settled, and with muffled anger, Phyllis waited for her mother's tca party.

The ladies came. Phyllis swallowed slippery complements from people who didn't know her, only polite words—raw oysters sliding down her throat. With each smile of greeting she pushed a load of resentment from her face, and by the time the afternoon was over, her cheek muscles ached.

●

Arthur tried to answer her when Phyllis asked how the day had been. "How—can—I—tell—a—perfect—day?"

"Maybe only a little of it."

"We—walked—by—the—river. We—walked—up—that—road—over—the—water."

"Over the high bridge in the park? Where the stream is narrow and deep? You 'walked' in your chair?"

"Yeah—walked—with—Mary. I—thought—I—might—fall—all—the—way—down. But—then—I—was—lifted—up—into—hope—and—joyfulness." Arthur seemed to be reaching beyond his human boundaries, and Phyllis knew he wanted to say more.

The following day he worked out his "song":

NEW DAY

Yesterday,
I walked by the river,
The river deep and calm.

Yesterday,
I looked out at the river,
The river brown and dirty.

As I looked, I feared I would slip and fall,
But then I felt I would crawl back out:
Just a baby chick from a dirty egg, another lump
of clay.

On this new day,
I walked over the river,
The river waved by the wind.

On this new day,
I looked down at the river,
The river blue and clean.

As I looked, I feared I was going to fall,
But then I knew I would rise again
Like a golden chick from an Easter Egg,
Another sun in the sky.

●

Although it was late, Phyllis knew that Arthur would not be asleep. She went into his room, stood beside his bed. The initial silence transformed to a tissue of small sounds that wrapped the night against the rumble of the city.

She sat on the edge of his bed. He turned his eyes to her. No other movement.

"If you could have any wish you wanted, what would it be?" she asked.

"I—want—to—feel—what—it's—like—to—be—born."

Phyllis put her hand on his arm, like warm wood.

"Would—you—do—something—for—me,…"

Phyllis did not wait for his *please*. "I suppose so."

"Move—my—bed." He indicated the window. "I—want—to—hear—the—night." His eyes were dark hollows, shaded from the new moon.

Phyllis stood. The brass bed was heavy; it had no casters.

She lifted the foot and then the head close to the open window, then rolled her brother to his side so that he could look into the night. She put a soft pillow between his bony knees. Steadily, under the whispcr of cars from the other side of the house, insects pulsed their skeletal songs under the cool stars.

"The—world—is—beating—its—heart"

Phyllis bent over the bed and kissed his cheek before she left the room.

●

Arthur lay quietly on his right side. Inside his head he felt a clear river washing away all the trivial stones in his mind, clearing the path in front of him. He could see his way. He felt a call, encouraging but, at the same time, an irresistible command as from a great mountain, its top out of sight. The way was beyond anything he could do, but his ambition was stronger than doubt so that the unattainable could be easy as the flight of Superman.

Arthur fixed his eyes on the base of the screen where it was torn from the frame. In this journey from the bed to the windowsill, his head must lead. All his mind concentrated on the first step—he must turn sideways across his bed, a test of every part of him. He made his first shuddering thrust, once, then again and again. But the edge of his mattress defied him. The sagging center trapped him away from the edge. Arthur lay tense and quivering with the after-shock of his exertion. His body, as though trapped between mountain peaks, mimicked aspen leaves trembling in the valley. He gasped for breath like a mountain climber in thin air. Finally, exhausted rest.

Next time he tried more slowly, thinking only of his shoulders. It worked. When he again rested, his head and neck extended over the edge of the mattress. With his chin on the windowsill, he could look up. He saw a path of stars, the giant spine of the sky pale, but brave, above the city lights. Its glow reached down to him; he smiled back.

The whole sky shined on his effort and lit his dream of

reward. He was ready to try again. This time the thorny edge of the screen raked the back of his neck and shoulders. He could feel a warm trickle of blood run down the right side of his neck.

I am a brave man. The danger below him sharpened his awareness and his control as well. Brave in his trust, he looked down at the dark ground and saw the stars. *Life is everywhere. I am alive for always and always.*

●

Phyllis's sleep centered her in pulsing light that spread slowly outward, and the shock of her feelings was cushioned in space. She saw a blue-white expanse like snow. Through the twilit hills, a wide track had been roughened by the passing of many feet. She woke feeling lost in space outside her mind, too frail and tiny for the bright morning.

Phyllis walked down the hall. She heard no morning steps and no soft-closing doors. No sound came from Arthur's day-room. Uneasy voices drifting through his window drew her into his bedroom, toward the bed pushed close against the window. She saw the screen: loose and bulging, ripped out across the bottom—She knew.

She walked toward the window, her steps slow and stiff with terror.

She knelt on the bed, compelled to look at what she feared. Like a brand, the image burned into her being—the hand, the stretch of arm reaching from rumpled blue pajamas; his mother standing beside the hand, her light dressing gown fluttering in the wind—lavender flowers, yellow centers, white background, her unpinned hair blowing loose.

I did it. The burning pain broke her paralysis and exploded her voice.

"Arthur," she shouted, "Arthur." She saw only the imprint on her mind of his immobile image as she rushed to be with him. Her mother was on the grass beside him holding his right hand. Phyllis sat by his head and looked down into his still face, a strange waxy gray. She leaned over him and tenderly ran her index finger across his cold forehead and down the side of his face, feeling the slight bristle of his whiskers so acutely that the sensation ran through her whole being. Her heart was a throbbing wound caught between the close memory of his life and the reality of his dead body beside her. Only her brother existed, yet he was gone. The immensity of her grief found no expression. There on the grass, time raced by or stood still; she could not tell the difference.

A siren blared. Phyllis heard it as though it existed in another world—until it stopped. Realizing its mission, Phyllis felt the gulf between his death and her warm life.

The approach of muted male voices jarred Phyllis from her shock. She stood up. Through a blur of tears she saw men in white jackets approaching around the corner of the house. She could not watch them take her brother away. Without seeing, she rushed past the paramedics toward the back door, bumping into the stretcher in her blind run.

Back on Arthur's bed, Phyllis straightened her legs and fell onto his blanket. She pressed her face into his pillow: soap, the same scent as in the vibrant night. With it she breathed in Arthur's life, all the actions he could not perform outside his mind—now this. Driven to look again at the sight she dreaded, she pushed herself up to her hands and knees. It just couldn't be real—bizarre hump of sheet like a polar bear in a formal garden, frozen winter on the sun-sparkled grass. Men in white jackets preformed their ceremony, bowing, lifting the covered form. They placed it on the stretcher, then crouched to the handles, rising, marching steadily away. The mother, a fluttering spectator in bedroom clothes misplaced.

When Phyllis looked through the window again, there was only grass; she felt her brother break away from her. She rolled to her back, and tears ran into her ears.

She knew without turning her head that her mother had come into the room. She felt the bed sag at the edge, the hand on her hair.

"Dear strange child." Such softness came, like a wandering foreigner, into her mother's voice. "Difficult, so difficult. I tried. Dear twisted body."

Phyllis felt her mother rocking back and forward on the bed. The sobs inside her mother clutched at Phyllis. Her mother's tense hand moved through Phyllis's tangled hair to her neck. It stopped, and Phyllis felt her mother's fingernails—*Arthur's fingers around the neck of the cat*... "Can't you let go of me!" as she exclaimed, Phyllis recognized the fear and guilt behind her angry snap. "I'm sorry," she said. "I know you really didn't mean to, and it didn't really hurt, but it made me remember..." She broke off with another apology. "I'm sorry."

Her mother stood up, mumbling. Phyllis repeated, "I'm sorry. It's not your fault."

She didn't seem to hear Phyllis. "Your father. He will be here soon. He should be here now. It is..." Her words faded as she walked down the hall.

Phyllis went into Arthur's day room, looked into the deep seat of his chair. She sat into the basket seat which held her folded in the middle and looked through his window. The leaves outside were moving, and the life of a squirrel waved through them, the movement Arthur only looked at. The cramping of his chair was hurting her, and Phyllis stood up.

As she came into the hall, she saw her father coming up the stairs. "Deirdre!" he called. She came out of her room, still in her dressing gown and with her hair straggling. He took his wife into his arms. It looked to Phyllis as though he were holding a rag doll.

She heard her mother repeating, "Why? Why? How could he do it?"

"Why what" Her husband's voice was firm. "Deirdre, please tell me what happened."

He waited, holding her up. In the pause before she spoke, it was as though her mind had blown away, and she was waiting to gather it back. "Last night I went into his room to say, *Good night* to him. It was beautiful and peaceful. He asked me to move his bed. *I did not do it. I did not do it!* But this morning his bed was tight against the window."

Phyllis stepped back into the doorway of her room, squeezed her elbows to her sides and clutched her wet face.

Her mother continued, "Such a strange accident!"

Mr. Dean had more questions. "But how could he have done it? I didn't know he ever rolled over by himself. He just isn't strong enough, and more than that, he would have had to turn, somehow thrash his way through that screen headfirst." Arthur's power of purpose was reflected in the horror that spread across his father's face; Phyllis felt her heart stripped bare, yet fear stopped her sobs.

His mother shook her head, disbelieving. "How could he have done it? But he has a tremendous amount of strength when he is angry, his tantrums can be really violent. What was he thinking? I so tried to give him all he needed."

"The screen should have been repaired. It was old; it was loose at the bottom. But I kept putting it off."

Mrs. Dean was rocking forward and back in her husband's arms. "In the last few weeks... Somehow in the last few weeks he seemed to be more peaceful, more relaxed," she said. "Not all the time. Only occasionally."

"Then you're saying that he was gaining a little control? Enough to roll, to thrust himself head first through that screen?"

"His little body..." But she had no answer, only shook her head. "Who...?"

Phyllis could not bring herself to answer her father's question. She stayed in the shadow of her doorway, and *I did it* remained a mute thought. *But Arthur did it too, with his will ...to die? Not on purpose, not on purpose. An accident, but more, how hard he had worked learning to hypnotize himself so that his muscles could let go! Yet this ability he was learning could not explain the purposeful movement he had used. Such a powerful will to die*—Phyllis felt again the white expanse of her dream, pulsing with light—*or to be reborn.*

Phyllis started to leave her room; but her mother stopped her. As she looked into her mother's face, she saw an understanding way beyond her expectations.

"Would you please help me?" Phyllis followed her mother to Arthur's sleeping room. She went to the head of the bed as her mother went to the foot. In a futile ritual they moved the bed back from the window. When it was done, their eyes met.

"It's hardly any lighter now," Phyllis whispered. Her sobs burst free. She felt her mother's arms around her and they wept together. "I didn't know!" she exclaimed through her tears.

"Of course you didn't. My dear, my dear, I know you only wanted to help him. You were so good to him, but I..." Her mother choked back her sobs, then went to her room to get dressed.

●

In the days that followed, time lost its mundane reality to Phyllis and became a strange blending of her life with an awareness of Arthur's spirit, a comforting presence that calmed her frequent fits of sobbing.

In a quiet interlude Phyllis sat at her desk looking out at Arthur's oak tree. Her mother asked from the doorway, "Phyllis, come. I would like to show something to you." She followed to her mother's room. "Here on the bed..." They sat beside each other. Her mother's small body, without the boundaries of a corset, seemed vulnerable. Between them was a flat object, tissue wrapped. Her mother folded back the paper. "Baby" in gold letters flowed across the cover. She opened the book. "Arthur: admirable, marvelous." The tiny foot print, page a little torn, mended with tape.

"You put the pages back!" Phyllis exclaimed

"Remember?" Their mother turned the page to the bent and broken feathers of the bird Phyllis had patched and pasted for her brother. "You were only nine, but see..." She gently stroked the feathers. "You were so careful; all of the feathers glued in the right direction. He loved it so. There was so little the poor boy could do." Phyllis watched her mother slowly and painfully shake her head. "It took me so many years to know," she murmured.

"It took me a long time too," Phyllis said, thinking of the limited surface which was all she had seen of her mother for so many years.

"He so wanted to be free. On his last night he asked me to move his bed, but I just could not do it." Phyllis watched her mother as, wonderingly, she stroked the bird's turquoise wing feather with her index finger. The pale-pink polish was a little chipped. "Arthur loved it so," she repeated.

"I didn't know," Phyllis said, "never imagined you'd keep all this."

"His story, 'The Little Bird,' I know it almost by heart. 'Someone put the little bird in a box. He fell two feet'." Her white head rocked. "Two stories to the ground, and his little neck was broken. Such a strange accident...Of course you could not have known. But his story—as if it was all decided, way back then." She closed the book. Neither one stood up.

"You knew so many things about him. I did not know how to reach you. I did not know how to ask..."

Phyllis could feel her mother's admiration.

●

The red letters of Northern States Power Company blinked from the invisible building below the hill, on and off, glaring through the night with monotonous insistency. With her chin resting on her fist, Phyllis watched from her desk chair. On and off. She would like to believe Arthur's death was all an accident. But with the next red blink she knew that her mother's need could not be hers. Arthur's death was Purpose, and somehow she would need to continue his strivings toward a free life.

Phyllis focused on the word *Power*, let it inside, felt it flash through her body and her mind, energy without purpose—at first. The purpose came through her recall of Edie's words as Mary quoted them: "Use the gift, or it will turn into something terrible." As though fear of inaction had replaced fear of action, Phyllis's plan came to her quickly and clearly.

She heard her father's step in the hall. She opened her door and called him. "Can I talk to you?"

He came into her room, stood beside her and looked out at the city lights. Phyllis was seeing her entire plan at once but was not yet ready to give it words.

Her father put his hand on his daughter's shoulder. "Phyllis, I want you to know that I deeply sympathize with what you are going through. Your mother and I don't blame you."

"I know. But I'm glad you're saying it. At first, all I wanted was to be dead with him. Now I don't feel so alone with it all."

"You're not alone. It's my guilt too, you know. I neglected the screen."

"But you didn't know."

He nodded, then continued. "Not alone at all! I can empathize more closely than you know." He lowered his head. "The years I struggled with my guilt over Tom's death... He would not even have been on Baffin Island were it not for me, and in the end, he called to me, and I delayed." His head was bowed. "Like you, I wanted to be dead with him."

Phyllis looked up at the sadness in his face. "You and Tom? It never crossed my mind. All I can think about is Arthur. I knew about that disastrous hunt like an old myth, a story somehow separated from real life. When I first heard it, you were too strong to me, beyond normal emotions."

Phyllis heard his chuckling laugh, felt his pat on her shoulder. "We're a lot closer to the same age now."

Phyllis turned from the window and looked up at her father. His face was dark in the gathering dusk. "I try to think it's not all bad," she said, "inevitable. It always happens. Death. I have no idea what that is, but for Arthur, I think he saw it more like birth, something good, a new adventure more exciting than the life he had. Maybe he was like you were, wanting excitement. Otherwise, why would he have done it when he wasn't depressed? He seemed so content that night, his time with Mary and all. As if life could never be better for him."

"Perhaps for Arthur nonliving is an extension of life. Some die within life; perhaps others live within death. But Tom, he saw so much ahead of him! He wanted all this life had to offer." His hand dropped from his daughter's shoulder.

Phyllis stood up and embraced her father. He smiled down at her. "Love mixes well with sadness."

Phyllis laughed a little.

"But you—" His face flickered in the red flashes from The Northern States Power Company. "You have a full life waiting. Arthur would want that for you."

Phyllis nodded her head against his chest. "I know that now. I want to live my life. But I think it was the way you said, 'Arthur lives in his dying'." Phyllis looked up into his face and saw his head nod. "Arthur taught me a whole lot—is teaching me even now. I can almost feel his life in me."

"None of us will ever forget him."

"Father, I have to ask you something. I have a plan for my life."

"Shoot."

"I have to get away from here. Not right away, but soon."

"Hold on there, you don't just run away, you go somewhere."

"I know. I have plans. I'm thinking I'll change my major from art and go into education at the U.—special education. It's like I'll be using what Arthur taught me. People do it all so wrong!"

"Wait a bit. We'll see."

"But I know." Phyllis trembled with purpose, with all she had not told him. Lips parted, she looked into his still face, his thoughts buried under sadness, or perhaps just the dim light. Perhaps a reluctant *no* was slowly making its way to his lips, and she had to stop it. "I *know!*" she repeated.

"Yes. I believe you do. I'll support whatever you decide," he said.

●

The day of the funeral had arrived. Mrs. Dean was down-stairs assisting in the arrangement of the flowers. Phyllis had finished making her mother's bed, but she did not leave the room; again she was drawn toward her mother's diary, com-pelled to know her better. She turned to the final dream, writ-ten just after Arthur's death:

> *"Then I was holding him under my arm: Arthur, and they gave him to me, dead. I was holding him clamped to my side, and he stuck out stiff like a stick. He did not weigh anything at all. I was just standing there on the platform, and I had to get him to the plane. The ticket taker was asking, 'What have you got there?' I was afraid. I was terribly afraid. I answered, 'My doll.' Then the ticket taker picked up the hand of the corpse. It was flat and gray and lined. Then he dropped the hand as though it were repulsive, obscene. Then he said, 'Some doll!'"*

Such horror about death! She must have drawn no comfort from her favorite poem:

> *"The Nerves sit ceremonious, like Tombs–*
> *The stiff Heart questions..."*

Phyllis's mind played pieces of a half-remembered poem by ee cumminngs:

> *"sweet spontaneous...the earth, and death the only love to which she will be true...Death, Earth's rhythmic lover, and she answers him with children of spring."*

Phyllis went down stairs into the heavy scent of too many flowers, colored dead, soon to be joined by the scent of too many perfumed people. Phyllis stood apart and watched her mother, as obedient to the laws of ceremony as the Queen of

England. Her hair was collected in its bone pins, and her voice played proper words, giving no hint of real emotion under that surface. *Mother feels so much. But on either side of birth and death, she sees a magnitude of fear.*

Just before the service, Mary and Phyllis stood alone and close together by Arthur's fern-covered casket. They spoke softly, almost in whispers.

"Arthur lived until he was... until he found his own kind of wisdom," Phyllis said, "He grew to his limit. His life was so little, and he didn't know where else he could go. He was finished. He was even happy that night, thanks to you, and then he could see beyond the end." Phyllis thought she saw a fuzzy ball of light rising up from his casket.

"As if he is lighting the way for each one of us," Mary said.

Phyllis nodded. "He wanted to know what it feels like to be born."

"Like reincarnation?" Mary questioned. "Edie believed that, but I don't quite trust it," Mary said. "I like this world too much the way I am."

"I guess I don't exactly understand it either. It's a lot to get my brain around."

"It's not something you think about. It's one of those things you just know—or else you don't. But it reminds me of something Edie told us one time," Mary said, "about a tribe of people who could choose their dying time. The old one would have a party when it was time to die. Then everyone in the tribe would come, and they would all tell him the same thing they said when he was born: 'I love you, and I support you on your journey'."

Mary looked out of the window, over the trees. "Next job I want to work with babies. But I'll be sorry to leave my people at the home. They can be happy and real funny too."

"I think Arthur would like me to work with your people— 'help them talk,' he said, 'I want everyone to know who I am'."

Mary wiped her eyes with the back of her hand and reached out to Phyllis. "It's real lonesome with Celeste gone and Timmy overseas. You can live with me."

They held each other until it was time for Phyllis to leave Mary and sit, for a short time, on the chair between her parents.

About the Author

The author lives with her husband in rural Afton, Minnesota.

Cynthia Davidson Bend, M.A. in human development, has taught young adults disabled by cerebral palsy. For eight years she facilitated writing with an ongoing group of students at The School for Social Development (now Partnership Resources).

She taught creative writing at Minnesota Metropolitan State University and has published *Birth of a Modern Shaman*, a biography, and short stories in literary journals. *Arthur's Room* is her first novel.